In the beginning there was Lana—
　　　And then there was Anna DeVoss

SUMMER, 1974

Chapter I

How could two or three weeks with an old woman in a place called Holy Rood Valley cure more than six years of pain and frustration? It was too much to expect or even to hope for. The hell with it! She shook her head and concentrated on the climbing road.

After the van ahead had crossed the narrow bridge and crept into the right lane of the four-lane segment of highway, Anna DeVoss shifted to third and stamped down on the accelerator, her long legs working in unison with her arms. The red Porsche shot ahead into the left lane, throwing Anna's head back against the headrest. She glanced toward her mother-in-law to see if she had been inconvenienced. Mrs. DeVoss stared straight ahead, a troubled look narrowing her eyes. Anna knew she was worrying about an older sister in a Jacksonville hospital.

Once past the van, she cut back into the right lane and slowed, climbing the eastern slope of the Appalachians at a more leisurely pace. Suddenly there was a tightness in her ears and she swallowed, clearing them. She turned her head occasionally, gazing through the huge bug-eyed sun shades at the green knolls and ridges as they swelled skyward to her right or dropped away to her left. Approaching three thousand feet, she could feel a change in the air, an unfamiliar coolness as the backwash swept past her left arm resting on the door.

Just before they climbed the final grade, before they ducked beneath the stone bridge of the Parkway and crossed the spine of the Blue Ridge at Deep Gap, Anna looked back to her left. The Appalachians rolled away toward the Piedmont to the south-east, blue and misty, ridge beyond ridge, mountain dome after mountain dome, fading out in haze along the horizon. The farthest range she could discern appeared higher than the Blue Ridge, but she knew it was an illusion. The mountains were actually stepping downward toward the foothills, toward the rolling landscape of the western North Carolina Piedmont and the flatlands beyond. From the highway east of Wilkesboro, the range she now crossed had climbed toward the sky, blue and hazy. But now, spreading around her, the slopes wore the brilliant green of early June. She and Pete had once driven along Skyline Drive, in western Virginia's modest contribution to the Appalachian range, but she had never been in mountains this rugged before. They subdued her. She had an urge to steer onto the right shoulder and hug the bank, away from the dropoff to her left. Yet there was a tranquility in being here that assuaged ever so slightly the old sadness hovering about the edges of her awareness. Beyond the Blue Ridge, the sensation of being in the mountains diminished, as she drove through rolling hills and farmlands and passed small roadside businesses.

The town of Boone, dominated by the highrise dormitories of Appalachian State University, lay along a narrow valley, spilling over hills and ridges to the east and west. They stopped at a huge old building of faded weatherboarding and ate lunch, served from dishes placed on their table, family style. Mrs. DeVoss nibbled at her food, her mind far away, but Anna ate with relish. The vegetables and stewed apples were especially delicious, probably because they had been seasoned with pork. Between bites, Anna would glance occasionally toward the stranger who was her mother-in-law, sympathizing with her, yet feeling inadequate because she knew of nothing she could say that would ease the worry of her companion. Maud DeVoss was a tall, slender woman with a gaunt but handsome face. Her nose was straight as a rifle barrel, the kind of nose her son had had. Anna had discovered in the last four days that the older woman could be talkative and pleasant company occasionally, but not today.

They left town, heading southwestward past green slopes with red wounds in them where bulldozers had gouged out bays for tourist shops and apartment houses. The highway was a two-lane strip of asphalt which climbed a gradual rise and then dropped steeply for a mile, passing chalets, an asphalt plant, and a campground, as it black-snaked its way downward into a meandering valley. Anna's gaze kept straying from the road, picking out rock formations, cone-shaped hills, and narrow valleys wandering away to the left and right. The Appalachians here were not blue, a darkling land, as the Cherokees had called them, but flaming green, an overwhelming green which soothed her and shut her away from the rush of the world she had left that morning.

She was startled when Mrs. DeVoss spoke. "You turn right just beyond that bridge ahead."

But she had already moved her foot to brake. She had known where to turn. Pete had brought her along this route more than once, in their conversations, although they had never found time to come here together. Never would find— She cut the thought short, like slicing a taut cord.

They followed the left bank of a swift little river for about two miles, most of the time beneath a dense canopy of trees. The narrow, winding strip of asphalt probably followed an old wagon road, which followed an older Indian trail, which in turn followed an even older buffalo trail. Pete had once told her that many of the mountain roads followed old animal trails, with the original curves and stream crossings still in them.

Mrs. DeVoss spoke again after they left the tunnel of trees and approached a huge, two-story building on the right, dark with age. There was a narrow little porch, two rusting gas pumps like two strangers standing close together for companionship, and a dilapidated farm wagon to one side, the mules hitched to it testing the sound of the approaching car with long ears swinging from side to side like hairy antennae. Anna could see faded signs on the side of the building: Peach Snuff, Rumford Baking Powder, B. C. Headache Powders, and Nehi Grape.

"That's Sparr's Store," Maud DeVoss said. "That's where the community trade and get their mail."

Anna glanced at her. The sadness had left her face briefly and was replaced by a pensive tranquility. She turned her head to study the old building as they moved past it. Anna wondered whether she was remembering the many times she had visited the store with her late husband or if she was recalling some specific occasion that had remained a pleasant memory.

Half a mile beyond the store, she veered to the left onto a dirt road, crossed a narrow, low-water bridge spanning the river, an iron grill cattle bridge beyond, and shifted to third, climbing at an angle to the right, the spur of the ridge. A one-strand electric fence ran along the base of the slope, which had been stamped into countless parallel terraces by the feet of generations of grazing cattle.

"That stream is the Watauga River," Mrs. De-Voss muttered, almost to herself, it seemed. "It empties indirectly into the Gulf of Mexico."

Anna glanced toward her again but said nothing. She followed a sharp curve back to the left, then turned to the right, climbing the gently rising slope. To her left, fifty yards away, a forest began in a straight line and stretched away toward the base of the ridge, to rise again in the distance, covering a higher knoll. Up ahead, the black shingled roof of a farmhouse came into view, beyond which she could see the tin roof of a barn and other outbuildings. Several Black Angus and white-faced cattle grazed off to her right, two of them raising their heads to stare indifferently at the approaching car, chewing slowly.

"That's the Webber place," Mrs. DeVoss said, pointing. "They own all the land around here." She paused, thoughtful. "Except, of course, the lots for the three summer places back in the woods."

A road branched off to the left, straight into the forest, and Anna could see the roof of an A-frame cabin with a glass front, partly concealed by trees. A short distance beyond, she turned left into a second road. She could not see the DeVoss chalet until she had passed a stand of young white pines and was suddenly in the yard, if the place could be said to have a yard. The drive ended in a loop circling tall oaks and poplars near the front door, four short parking bays perpendicular to the house front. Anna pulled into the one nearest the front steps and switched off the engine.

For several seconds she and the older woman sat in silence, as Anna studied the building. It was built of hewn logs, black with age, logs, Pete had once told her, that Dr. DeVoss had obtained from an old barn some native had sold him. The architecture was rectangular, the steep roof covered with cedar shakes, the eaves at right angles to the driveway. A stone chimney was built against the near side of the cabin, a door to the right of it and a window to the left. Even the cement chinking between the logs seemed darkened by time, with here and there patches of moss or lichen splotching it like creeping blight.

"Well, this is Greenworld." Mrs. DeVoss looked at her and smiled. "How do you like it?"

Anna stared straight ahead. She tried to visualize a young Pete DeVoss, barefoot and in shorts, brown as an Indian, shinnying up the trees or scurrying away among them. "It's lovely," she said softly. "It's—it's out of my world. It's wonderful."

When Mrs. DeVoss reached for the handle of the door, Anna opened her own. She unfolded from the deep bucket seat and towered above the top of the Porsche. Her knees cracked, loud in the silent forest. There was a catch in her back. She braced her hand against the top of the car, her balance awry. The long ride had molded her into one position too long. A moment later, she hurried around the car. She opened the other door and grasped Mrs. DeVoss's hand, helping her out and to her feet. The older woman tottered a moment, but quickly adjusted to standing.

Anna followed her up the hewn-log steps onto the deck of the chalet. By the time they had reached the door, Mrs. DeVoss had a bunch of keys in her hand and unlocked the door. Despite the light from several windows, Anna had to peer and blink rapidly, coming from the bright outer light into the gloom. She removed her sunglasses and looked about her. There was a slight taint of mustiness in the air, a closeness resulting from the fact that the cabin had been shut up for several months without ventilation, but the odor was not unpleasant. It gave her a feeling of nostalgia, a sense of old things long unused, which results in a gentle sadness.

On her left, dominating the front of the cabin, was a large stone fireplace with raised hearth and a stone mantel. Above it hung a painting framed with wormy chestnut. She studied it briefly. Several little men and women dressed like Pilgrims frolicked in a wood, one of their children riding a reddish-brown squirrel along a rotting log. Comfortable looking leather-padded chairs sat tranquilly in front of the fireplace, four of them, once black but now scarred and faded. They reminded Anna of old men drawn together for a quiet conversation, but momentarily silent. A black bearskin rug sprawled between the chairs and the hearth, the head snarling toward some unseen enemy across the room.

The right end of the cabin consisted of two bedrooms, a bathroom separating them. The rest of the interior was cathedral, including the fireplace and living area and the kitchen-dining area. The left end of the building contained a sink beneath double windows. There were an electric stove, a refrigerator, and a lazy-Susan table, with ladderback chairs marshaled around it. Between the living area and the far wall was a reading area, crowded bookcases lining the wall and rearing ceilingward between two windows. There was no radio, no television, not even a telephone that Anna could see.

"The master bedroom is the farther one there," Mrs. DeVoss explained, as they crossed the oak floor. "You take it, since you'll probably be here longer than I will. It's larger than the other, and the double bed will give you sprawling room."

Anna stopped in front of the bathroom door. "No! No, don't let's do that. I don't want to deprive you of comfort. I can switch rooms if you have to leave earlier."

Mrs. DeVoss touched her lightly on the shoulder, smiling tiredly. "Don't argue with me, child. I know what's been going on inside you since we left

Arlington. At least I think I do. The room is yours. That settles it."

Anna hesitated, but could think of no further argument. "All right, then." She turned to the left, toward her bedroom. "You're the boss."

Inside, she stared about her. A huge four-poster bed sat in the far corner to her right, a patchwork quilt serving as a spread. Matching the bed, an antique dresser of red cherry stood against the wall close by to her left, and a matching chest of drawers reared upward on her right, beside the door. A Boston rocker with splint-bottom and back waited in the corner farther to her right, a reading lamp peering over the left shoulder of whatever ghost occupied it at the moment. At the right end of the cabin, double windows permitted a view of the gently rising slope of the ridge. A single window beside the bed looked out onto the back deck of the cabin.

She crossed the oval hooked rug, placed her right knee on the window seat, and raised the window beside the bed. Immediately, the room was filled with a lulling, liquid murmur from down the slope and to the right. She had known the waterfall would be there, but it caught her by surprise when it asserted itself on the silence. The window opened onto the screened sleeping deck, and beyond it, the slope fell gently through a maze of columns whose green tops reared from sight somewhere above the roof. Below the intrusion of the waterfall, Anna could vaguely hear the flutter of a stream over and around rocks somewhere in the woods farther down the slope.

"Besides, you can hear the falls better from this room."

Anna whirled. Mrs. DeVoss stood just inside the door, a hand braced against the door facing. "I was already alone in a strange world," Anna laughed. "You startled me."

"The waterfall is an added blessing," the older woman said. "It is a balm for sadness, although there's something—something sad about the sound of it. You will go to sleep hearing it, and you will wake up hearing it, and it will be a calm voice assuring you everything will be all right." Mrs. DeVoss was not looking at Anna. She was staring above the bed at a large photograph of a young man and woman in wedding clothing. "We spent every summer in this room for thirty-nine years," she continued, "except part of one in Austria. I have been here forty-one—since the summer of 1933."

"It—it's a peaceful room," Anna said, not knowing what else to say. "I'm sure I'll enjoy it."

Mrs. DeVoss turned and left the room quickly. Anna heard the bathroom door close, and she was left alone.

After Anna had carried their bags in, placing them in the respective bedrooms, Mrs. DeVoss still had not left the bathroom. Once Anna started to knock on the door, hesitated, then let her arm drop. Without any clear direction, she went out onto the back deck. She crossed it, thrust open the screen door and descended the steps. The straight boles of yellow pines and poplars towered upward, blotting out the sky, except for a swatch of blue here and there. A path led down the side of the ridge, but away from it the forest was almost clear of undergrowth. She could hear the gush of the waterfall even more clearly outside here, and the cool of the forest settled about her, denying the existence of an afternoon sun.

As she descended the meandering path, her sandals made soft swishing sounds now and then to break the silence of the forest. Ferns grew in isolated beds on both sides of the trail. A mossy boulder reared up suddenly in front of her. Rounding it, she reached the banks of the rushing stream ten feet beyond. The path crossed the creek on two stepping-stones and continued onward, but a tributary path traced the left bank, upstream. She followed it, her eyes on the splashing water, and reached the flowers before she knew they were there. When she raised her eyes suddenly, she stopped, her lips parted in surprise. A jungle of Rosebay rhododendron stretched away from the right bank, their long, leathery leaves gleaming like metal in the forest twilight. But they were overshadowed by thousands of pink flowers, round clumps of them, reaching out of sight and covering the surface of the shrubbery like a brilliant froth.

Anna had never seen rhododendron in bloom before. She stood there staring, a little-girl look of delight and surprise softening the fatigue about her mouth and eyes. Back of her seeing was a symphony of odors, none of which she could identify other than to suspect that they were a blend of gifts from the forest, just as was the gush of the waterfall, somewhere close by.

Anna was startled back to awareness when some kind of bird, perhaps a woodpecker, leaped from a tree behind her, its wings drumming the air as it darted off into the forest, uttering shrill cries. She turned and looked after it, then followed the path farther upstream, the waterfall growing louder with each step. The stream and path looped back to the left around a peninsula of rhododendron. She rounded it and suddenly there it was.

The brook leaped over the brim of a low granite escarpment and arched out, then plunged into a deep pool beneath, foaming like champagne. The drop was not more than ten or twelve feet, but the flashing white scimitar of water gave Anna the impression of a greater distance. The pool was surrounded by a flat crescent of granite which on her side slid gradually beneath the pool, climbing to a garden of moss adjacent to the woods.

Kicking off her sandals, she waded into the pool, but stopped ankle deep, at the utter coldness of the water. She squatted and ruffled her fingers along the surface, then stopped again to let it calm.

She studied her reflection, almost as clear as a mirror. Her face in the water was bracketed by her knees. She brought her knees together and tugged at the hem of her short skirt, a mother-induced gesture of modesty. A sudden flicker of motion caught her attention. Three feet away, two fish, probably brook trout, darted away from her, the shadow of one chasing the shadow of the other along the pebbled bottom.

Walking backward onto the rock, Anna sat down beside her sandals. The sun-warmed rock added a comfortable glow to her buttocks through her skirt. At that moment she noticed the butterflies—black and gold, yellow, pale blue and orange—hanging close to the falling water, rising and drifting downward on beating wings as though drinking the mist that hovered just above the falls. Butterfly Falls, that was what Pete had called them. Now she could see why. She lay back, her hands clasped beneath her head, and stared upward at the splotches of sky showing through the canopy of pines and spruce towering over her. She relaxed against the warm granite, her breathing long and slow. For the first time that day she was aware of how weary she really was.

Day before yesterday at Arlington Cemetery— today, seven long hours from Norfolk to Greenworld in Watauga County. She closed her eyes. Far away, her memory echoed rifle shots in unison and the mournful sound of TAPS. A flag was folded expertly, revealing the utilitarian shape of the vault it had covered. A colorful triangle of fabric was thrust into the hands of the young woman in the dark suit, shattering her brown study. She stared from the flag to the officer as though wondering what to do with it. Then the scene shuttled forward like a silent movie skipping frames, and the couple, the young woman and her older companion, were wading through the forest of white crosses, leaving the metal cubicle behind—the cubicle she was expected to believe held the decayed remains of the young buck she had once held in her arms. She had looked back once and had felt nothing, no rapport with broken bones and fabric. Although the military was sure—the identification was beyond doubt—Anna DeVoss had not felt that the remains of her mate were stored in that metal cubicle. Her mind had known and had accepted the obvious, but her heart could not believe. She herself had not seen the bones of Pete DeVoss. His boyish grin, his muscular body, after six years, were still too real for her to let go. The last notes of TAPS faded, faded, and the two women merged into the green hillside, disappearing.

Anna awakened suddenly, shivering. A chilly breeze swept across her, fluffing the hem of her skirt. In the distance she heard the roar of the plane hurtling earthward. She sprang to a seated position, staring about her. It was only the roar of the waterfall. Her heartbeat slowed. She could see little flecks of the sun through the pines to the west. She checked her wristwatch. It was after six. Buckling on her sandals, she got to her feet and returned down the stream, along the rocky path. Once, she glimpsed a little man in dark knickers and silver buckles on his shoes and wearing a Pilgrim hat, as he sat on a rock stroking a squirrel almost as large as himself. But when she squinted to get a better look, only the squirrel was visible. Or had it been the ghost that lived in her brain that had seen it, the ghost that sometimes talked to her?

Mrs. DeVoss, busy in the kitchen, looked at her curiously when she entered the cabin, but said nothing. Anna entered her room, removed her robe and mules from one of the open bags, and went into the bathroom. She took off her halter, skirt, and half-slip and was ready to shower. She stood for a long time letting the fine jets of water pepper her shoulders, back, and breasts. It felt so soothing, she almost went to sleep, standing with her hands braced against the shower walls. After a while she slid back the shower panel and began to towel herself, rubbing until the flesh of her arms and torso turned a healthy red. She stepped out onto the bath mat to dry her legs and was startled when she caught a sudden movement out of the sides of her eyes.

Anna whirled, towel covering her lower body,

and had to laugh when she saw the tall young woman staring at her with open mouth, out of the full-length mirror on the back of the bathroom door. She stopped, finishing up first one foot, then the other, as she watched her movements in the mirror. She walked to within a couple of feet of the door and studied her reflection critically. At five feet, nine, she appeared taller than she actually was because she was so slender. But her hips were feminine and the slight dome of her belly did not require a girdle. There was no sign she had ever worn a bathing suit. She did not tan easily and had never been a fanatic about the fad, although she had spent countless sunny days at Virginia Beach over the years. She looked at her breasts, cupping her right hand to lift the right one slightly and feel it for any suspicious lump. They were not overly large and were as white as her belly.

Anna studied her face. At twenty-four, it was still young and pretty, except for dark shadows under the light blue eyes—under the gray eyes. At the moment they were gray, reflecting the moroseness that had lived inside her for the last several days. When she smiled suddenly—Pete had always accused her of grinning like a school kid—her eyes turned light blue. Her brown hair, with highlights of gold, was cut in a shag, and her nose was small and neat. She had learned long ago that it was her mouth that men noticed first. Her lips were full and sensuous, her lower lip slightly fuller than her upper. Her thick black brows seemed devised to steal the attention from her mouth.

Donning the robe and mules, she joined Mrs. DeVoss at the lazy-Susan table where they ate a dinner her mother-in-law had prepared from cans. The meal passed mostly in silence, and Anna washed the dishes afterwards while Mrs. DeVoss bathed. It was still light outside when Anna told her companion good night and entered her bedroom, closing the door. She sat for a while, trying to read a short story from a collection she had taken from the bookcase, but the words kept blurring and running across the page like speckled amoebae under a microscope. Above the muted buzz and tinkle of nocturnal insects, the quiet roar of the waterfall intruded on her awareness.

Twilight had just begun to sift down through the canopy of foliage sheltering the cabin when Anna drew back the covers, removed her robe, and stretched out on the bed. She could smell the faint mustiness of the bed covers, unused for a year, and could feel a gentle wave of air enter the open window and sweep across her body, stirring her hair, cooling her. God, but she was weary! She let her muscles relax and collapsed inward into herself, breathing evenly. The firm mattress was comfortable, sustaining her weight with authority. Her chest rose and fell. Her mind was a huge house with many lighted windows. Someone was running through the house from room to room switching off the lights. Finally, only two lights were left, then one. She did not know when that light was turned off. The house remained dark, but some area of her mind was aware that she became chilly during the night, arousing her defenses enough so that she covered herself with a sheet and blanket, leaving the patchwork quilt thrown aside.

Chapter II

She was back at UNC, and a neighbor was calling her, waking her for her first class. Bess must be outside the apartment calling me through the window, her mind reasoned, because her voice is muted. No, it could not be Bess. It's a man's voice. It's Pete calling me. He's back from a flight, back from Vietnam, back from—No! Not that word. But it had to be Pete. What other man would call her from her sleep?

Anna sat up in bed, her hands leaping to cover her ears, her eyes wide with fear. Then she calmed, orienting herself. She tilted her head to listen. There came another series of loud knocks on the front door, followed by silence. Then a man's voice, muffled by the intervening doors and walls, called again. "Maud! Maud! Hey, Maud, wake up, please ma'am!"

Slipping to the floor, Anna seized her robe, flung it around her, tying the sash with fingers still half asleep, and opened her bedroom door. She paused in the doorway, uncertain, then hurried across the cabin on her bare feet toward the front of the house.

She opened the front door and stared at Jesus Christ, Superstar, who stood two feet away, fist raised to knock again. The first object to catch her attention was the mop of golden kinky hair and the next was the cropped, kinky beard, parted at the center of the chin like a Spartan warrior's. The surprised eyes stared back at her, a flecked amber. The narrow mask of face between the mustache and hair was peppered with freckles, as were the upraised fist and forearm.

Why she should have been surprised at the appearance of a stranger she could not say, but surprise was chiefly what she felt at the moment. "Yes, what could I do for you?" she demanded.

For a few seconds longer he stared at her face, then let his eyes shift to include the rest of her. "I need to see Maud," he said. "I have a message for her."

"Maud?" Anna stared at him, her mind blank. "Oh, yes, you mean Mrs. DeVoss," she said, suddenly understanding.

For a moment the man appeared flustered. "Yes, Mrs. DeVoss." His shallow little laugh might have been a slight apology or a punctuation sound. "I've always called her *Maud*. Known her since I was a kid."

Anna could not have guessed his age with a gun to her head. He wore faded, patched jeans, the kind a beatnik might wear—or a farmer—a faded plaid shirt, and ragged sneakers without socks.

They eyed each other a moment longer in silence. Then the young man took a step backward, retreating.

"I'm Jay Webber," he explained, his solemn frown proof of identification. "We own the farm." He waved his arms to include the surrounding world, then abandoned it, letting it fall.

"Oh, yes!" she said. "Maud—Mrs. DeVoss is still asleep. I'll get her."

She left him standing on the deck and hurried toward Mrs. DeVoss's bedroom door. But before she reached it, Maud DeVoss appeared, a pink robe about her.

Anna stopped. "There's a young man here," she said. "He says his name is Webber. Says he has a message for you."

"Yes, that'll be Jay Webber." Mrs. DeVoss was looking beyond her, blinking sleepily. "Jay, do come in!" she called as she approached the front door. "Don't stand out there like you were a stranger."

Anna turned to watch Jay Webber enter the cabin and meet Mrs. DeVoss, hug her. "When did you grow that beard?" she asked. "I swear, it's hard to tell what you'll do next. I bet your daddy would have made you shave it off."

His laugh was casual. "Just got tired of shaving," he said. "Don't think about it much anymore unless somebody mentions it."

He had a slow, folksy drawl, a manner of speaking Pete had sometimes imitated when teasing Anna.

"This is my daughter-in-law, Anna, Jay." Mrs. DeVoss nodded toward her. "Jay is our neighbor and handy man—looks after the cabin when we're away and keeps everything working when we're here."

"Howdy, ma'am." Jay Webber bowed ever so slightly. Anna had a feeling the gesture was exaggerated.

"Good to meet you," she said. "Please excuse me." She returned to her bedroom, closing the door after her.

When she re-appeared later, dressed in yellow shorts and a white blouse, she found Mrs. DeVoss seated by the fireplace, sobbing silently. Anna approached her, hesitated, then placed a hand on the other woman's shoulder. "Do you want to talk to me about it?" she asked softly.

Mrs. DeVoss sat up straight, wiping at her eyes with her fingers. Without glasses on, her eyes were pits of blue wrinkles. "It was a call from Cousin Dinnah," she said. "Mable is worse—critical. I—I must go to her. Would you please drive me to the Greensboro Airport?"

"I'm so sorry," Anna said. "Certainly. We'll get you packed, and I'll have you there in no time."

Maud DeVoss was quiet all the way down and

out of the mountains, staring ahead through her heavy lenses, her mind apparently already in Jacksonville. After they had passed Wilkesboro and were tracing the rolling hills of the Piedmont, she said, "Stay in the cabin as long as you like, Anna. All summer, if it suits you. The mountains will calm you after those long years of—of waiting, not knowing for sure whether Pete—It's strange what a healthy perspective the mountains can give one who is used to living in hellish traffic and hubbub. After a while up there alone, you can see what has happened to you in a different light. You can—can come to accept things as they are."

For a moment Anna was embarrassed. Although Maud DeVoss had not turned to look at her, she felt trapped by her scrutiny, as though her companion had been reading her mind for the last three days. She had never discussed how she felt about Pete, missing in action, with her mother-in-law or anyone else because her feelings were so confused and personal she could not have analyzed them abstractly, let alone put them into words. They had hardly discussed husband and son at all on the way to and from the military funeral, both of them skirting the subject as though it were something obscene and unmentionable.

"Thank you, Maud," she said. "I'll stay awhile. It is peaceful at Greenworld." She paused. "I do hope your sister improves."

"It's not likely. It's terminal cancer. It's just a matter of enduring it to the end."

As they approached Friendship Airport, Anna felt a loss, regret that she had never got to know her mother-in-law any better than she had. The short military life she had spent with Pete had not permitted it, and after his carrier had sailed for Vietnam, after he had gone down on his second mission, she had been too busy losing herself in school to join her in-laws at Greenworld or to visit them in Jacksonville. Once, she and Pete had spent three days with them. Then, when Dr. DeVoss had died, she remained four days with her mother-in-law, but it was hardly a time to get well acquainted. Now, she felt as though she were losing an old friend—an old friend she never got to know at all, never would know.

When they embraced just before Maud DeVoss boarded her plane, the two women wept briefly and quietly, but for different reasons. Maud De-Voss, Anna guessed, for her dying sister, because she had long ago accommodated herself to the loss of her son and husband. But Anna DeVoss wept because she was losing someone she never had, the mother of her husband, a woman she might have grown to love and confide in, but never would know, now. Somehow, she was certain of that. If, or whenever they met again, it would be under different emotional circumstances, a young and an old woman passing in the daytime, pausing to exchange platitudes.

When Anna returned to Holy Rood Valley, around 2:00 P.M., she pulled into the graveled parking area in front of Sparr's Store. She was dying of thirst, but more importantly, she needed to buy a few things. Climbing the steps to the tune of creaks, she opened the rusty screen door and entered a cavernous room as gloomy as a barn loft. Huge windows at either end of the long building were glazed by decades of dust which daylight penetrated grudgingly. Her nose was assailed by many odors, some of them familiar, some of them, but not all, pleasant in a nostalgic way—new leather, ground coffee, raw plug tobacco. She was stopped by the sudden silence. Three old men sat around the huge round stove which dominated the center of the store like a totem, as though they had been left over from last winter, still talking about the old times. They had hushed when she came in, mouths half open, staring at her with friendly curiosity.

Anna stood a moment longer, blinking through her huge octagonal sun glasses as her eyes adjusted to the gloom. Finally, she removed them and dropped them into her handbag. As she paced forward slowly, stalking her audience, uncertain as to how to break the silence, one of them braced his hands against his knees and got slowly to his feet. Unlike the other two men, he wore khaki pants, with a white shirt and blue polkadot bowtie. He was a little man, hardly as tall as Anna, with a shining, florid face and a wing of graying brown hair combed across his pate. He grinned, showing a gold canine tooth, and nodded rapidly, then shuffled forward with outstretched hand.

"You must be Mrs. DeVoss, young Pete's widder," he beamed, pronouncing the Mrs. as *Mizeries.* "I'm Henry Sparr."

Anna stared at him in surprise, then took the cool, dry little hand. "Yes, I'm Anna DeVoss," she said. "But how did you know?"

Henry Sparr laughed a cackling laugh. "I'm the local know-it-all," he grinned. "I know everything that goes on in Holy Rood Valley, like my pa and my grandpa before me." He paused to study her reaction, apparently. When she did not respond, he continued, "No, I'll tell you the truth, Annar. Jay Webber come by today and mentioned that you and Maud was at the DeVoss cabin. The way he described you, I couldn't a-missed. That boy's got a sharp eye for things is purty."

For a moment Anna felt a surge of resentment toward one Jay Webber, hillbilly Paul Revere, then forgot him. She was a little surprised at how quickly the old man had seized her first name as a familiar tool. But she supposed it was a mountain custom which allowed a young Jay Webber to call her mother-in-law *Maud,* instead of *Mrs.*

"Annar, this here is Grove Miller," Henry Sparr said, as one of the other two men, tall and angular, stood and extended his hand. He wore a blue denim shirt under his overalls and a battered black felt hat.

"Proud to make your acquaintance, Annar," Grove Miller said. "Pete DeVoss was a fine young feller, and Dr. DeVoss was a angel." He pronounced it DE-voss.

His hand was calloused and rough as torn sandpaper to Anna's touch. "How do you do, Mr. Miller?" she said.

"And this here'n is Lem Perkins."

The third man reminded Anna a lot of Grove Miller, except for his straw field hat. "Howdy," he nodded and smiled, then sat back down. Anna was aware that he was trying not to look directly at her legs, below her shorts, but he yielded to temptation at the last moment, before tilting his head and staring at the dark rafters.

"Would you like to see my store?" the store-keeper asked. "Folks has come here from Canady all the way to Cubie and bought stuff. Been here on this spot for eighty-nine year."

Anna looked about her again. It was straight out of the nineteenth century, except for the lights dangling on long, black wires from the rafters and an ancient frigidaire behind the counter, in the far corner. Even the cash register was antique. A glass showcase stretched along one wall close by. Boxes of buttons, spools of thread, pocket knives, and boxes of striped stick candy could be seen through the scratched glass.

"This room ain't all of it," Henry Sparr explained, when she hesitated. "This here is jest the main part."

"Why—why, I would like to see it, Mr. Sparr," she said. "It's an interesting place."

She followed him through a gap between the wooden and glass counters and up some steps into a wing of the huge old building. They passed a stairway on the right leading up higher and entered another room, darker than the main store. Farm tools were scattered about the room, cluttering the floor and leaning against the walls. Anna recognized hoes, shovels, and pitchforks. Three or four kinds of plows were sitting here and there. Henry Sparr grasped the handle of one of them and turned toward her, grinning.

"I bet you a purty you don't know what this here is."

"It's a—a plow." She wondered if he really thought she was too stupid to know.

"Yeah, it's a plow, all right. But what manner of plow?" His grin broadened.

"I don't know. I grew up on a dairy farm, but I didn't plow much."

"It's a 13 Oliver-Chill. Best two-hoss plow in

these parts. Made right over the mountains there, in Chattanoogie, Tennessee."

Anna hesitated, wondering what the catch was. "Yeah," she nodded finally, "it's a fine looking plow, all right."

"I bet you don't know what them things is."

He was peering upward. She tilted her head and saw several old horse collars hanging from nails driven into the overhead beams. "They look like horse collars," she said.

"They are. They are," he affirmed. "They truly are. I bet you can't guess what I'm doing with used hoss collars."

"I can't imagine," she said, hesitating. "Unless you put them on used horses."

He laughed, throwing back his head, then slapped her on the back, staggering her. Briefly, she felt a surge of resentment at his familiarity. "That's funny. Used hosses. Nope, they's another reason. Them Floridy tourist folks buy'em and put looking-glasses in'em."

"Put *what* in them?"

"Looking-glasses!" He stared at her in puzzlement. "You know, mirrors."

"Oh, mirrors. You mean they really put mirrors inside used horse collars?"

"That they do." He rubbed his hands together, chuckling. "That makes them antiques. Anything that's a antique, they can hang on their parlor wall, even if it's a used hoss collar with a looking-glass in it."

Anna laughed, amused at the old storekeeper's sense of humor. And she was flattered in a way. Obviously, he considered her a flatlander too smart to hang horse collar mirrors on her parlor wall, just as he considered the DeVoss family separate from the typical tourists.

"Come on." He took her by the arm and escorted her back toward the door through which they had entered. "You ain't seen everything yet by a long shot. My grandpa built this store back around 1885. Runned it all his life. My pa runned it all his life, post office, too. I've worked it bout all my life, and you want to know somethin'? I got a boy that's a lawyer, and he ain't inter-rested in runnin' it. Reckon I'll jest have to get shet of it, when I run down."

They climbed the shadowy steps higher and entered a great sprawling room beneath the eaves. She stifled a cough, assailed by the tight dustiness of the air, air flavored by spicy smells she could not identify. The four small windows about the walls supplied more light than the larger windows downstairs. Around the perimeter of the floor, close to the sloping roof, lay piles of dark roots and what appeared to Anna to be chips of decaying bark. The center of the room was occupied with at least two dozen hand-made, split-bottomed chairs, both ladderback dining chairs and Boston rockers. In the far corner to her left sat a long, dark box that looked like a casket.

"I bet you a purty you don't know what that stuff is." Henry Sparr pointed to the dark piles along the edge of the room.

"It looks to me like roots and bark," she said.

He squinted at her. "Now how did a young lady like you figure that out?"

"Well," she was puzzled at his surprise, "that's just what it looks like."

"And that's precisely what it is. We used to take in roots and herbs. Up here's where we stored'em at. That stuff there was left over after we stopped shipping them out. It's jest laid there year after year not botherin nothin, and I've let it be."

"And I suppose," Anna laughed, "you're going to tell me that thing over there—" She pointed. "—is a coffin."

"That hit is!" Henry Sparr chuckled. "Grandpa sold everything from baby cradles to coffins. That'un is the only one we got left. Still belongs to old Sandy MacTavish. Belongs to his heirs, I reckon. But they ain't never spoke for it."

"Why didn't Mr. MacTavish use it?"

"Now that's a long story. He did use it, but not in the usual manner." Henry Sparr studied her solemnly, but there was a twinkle in his eyes. "Old Sandy studied dyin about all his livelong life, nearabouts. He had that coffin made out of black locust planks cause that wood don't never hardly rot in the ground. Black locust trees don't grow too big around, but Sandy had him some little planks sawed out anyways, even if they was narrer. He had Grandpa's coffin maker, Jed Hackett, to make the coffin to Sandy's measure, which was purty big. Sandy used to come up here onct or twict a month and lay back in his coffin and sing 'When the Roll Is Called up Yander.' Folks never knowed was he drunk, crazy, or what. You ask me why he didn't use it finally at last. That's the strangest part of all. Old Sandy was drowned in the 1916 fresh, and his body wasn't never found."

Anna's first impulse was to laugh at Sandy Mac-Tavish's frustrated plans for eternity. An image of the pomp and circumstances in Arlington Cemetery crossed her mind, and it was no longer funny. She was suddenly sad for old Sandy.

"Let's go back downstairs," she said. "It's spooky up here."

Henry Sparr stopped behind the old cash register, stooped, and lifted a small door in the floor under the counter. He looked at Anna and grinned. "I bet you a purty you can't guess what this here door was used for."

Anna shook her head. "No. I can't guess. Did you drop trash through, beneath the house?"

"Nope, but you're a gettin warm. We used to take chickens in trade from folks hereabouts. Pa built a fence around the store outside and used the underneath space for a chicken lot. One day he decided it would be easier and save time if he cut him a hole in the floor, here, and dropped the chickens through instead of totin'em outside and around to the door of the lot."

"Sheer genius," Anna laughed. "Your pa was a smart man."

She turned to watch Grove Miller behind the wooden counter. He had taken a roll of bologna and a huge wedge of cheese from the refrigerator and was making a sandwich, cutting thick slices of bread from what looked like a homemade loaf. He smeared the bread with mayonnaise and placed a slice of the meat and a slice of the cheese between the bread. Anna's mouth was suddenly full of saliva. Her stomach was a void demanding attention. She remembered she had had neither breakfast nor lunch. As she swallowed, she was convinced that nothing in the world could satisfy her hunger but a sandwich exactly like the one Grove Miller was just biting into.

She turned to the storekeeper. "Mr. Sparr, could I please, please make me a sandwich like that?"

"Hep yourself. Hep yourself," he grinned. "Jest a quarter. My old womern baked the bread jest yesterdy."

Anna sat in a chair by the cold iron stove and ate the best sandwich she had ever put in her mouth, drinking a cold orange drink between bites. Henry Sparr and Grove Miller sat facing her, grinning. Lem Perkins had left while she and the store-keeper were upstairs.

"Yep, the DeVosses was the first summer people to build in the valley," Henry Sparr stated. "Summer folks had been comin to Blowing Rock and Linville for years on end. Course, Linville is not in this county. We was let purty much alone out here, raisin our own corn and cabbages and Burley tobacker and stuff. One day Dr. DeVoss and Maud comes through in their Lasalle. That was before young Pete was borned. They stopped here and set in to talkin to J.W. Webber, happened to be at the store. I never seen two grown men take to each other so quick-like. Dr. DeVoss, a rich surgeon from Jacksonville, Floridy, and J.W., a mountain tobacker farmer didn't finish the fifth grade. Before the doctor had left, J.W. had sold him a acre of land for a summer house right up there in the woods nearabouts at Butterfly Falls. Sold it to him for chickenfeed, nearabouts. Dr. DeVoss had the log house built that same fall. Must a been 1931–32."

Grove Miller swallowed the bite he was chewing, almost choking on it. "It was 1932, Henry. I recollect it was the year before Roosevelt tuck over."

"Yeah. I believe you're right. I believe it was 1932." He looked at Anna. "Say you was brung up on a dairy farm?"

Caught between bites, she was not able to answer at once. "Yes, Princess Anne County, in Virginia. Between Norfolk and what was then Virginia

Beach. It's part of the City of Virginia Beach now. My father kept his farm going after almost all those around him had sold theirs for housing developments."

"I can understand that." The storekeeper shook his head. "A feller does the same thing all of his life, he dreads to give it up for new ways."

"Never will forget the time Dr. DeVoss operated on J.W. with a straight razor," Grove Miller said, looking at the stove. "Wasn't there my ownself, but everbody heard tell of it. After a thunderstorm the lights was out and the river was up. J.W. picked sech a time to have a pendicitis attack. He might nigh died, it was so sudden. Onliest thing saved him was Dr. DeVoss operated on him with a straight razor on the kitchen table underneath a lamp and a lantern light. Dr. DeVoss and J.W. sucked through the same quill from then on."

"Yeah," the storekeeper agreed, "the DeVosses tuck the time to stop and go easy and live slow, like us folks that growed up here. Nowadays, summer folks has got to have two or three big, fancy cars amongst a family and drive from here to yander lookin for entertainment—auctions of junk and tourist show places and eatin at them little old hamburger stands with red roofs scattered along the roads, set back in red clay notches gouged in the green hillsides, so much alike, a big old hen might as well a-laid them all. And lots of them want to buy all the land right out from underneath everybody. They can't take pleasure in lookin at the mountains and the rocks and the trees. They've got to own them. I recollect how well the DeVoss family fitted into the community back yander and how most of the folks hereabouts liked them and never thought about them being big, rich folks from way down there in Flordy."

Anna took her last bite, chewing slowly, relishing it while regretting it was all she wanted. She swallowed the remainder from her drink bottle, studying the old men beneath lowered lashes. She wondered if they were telling her all this because they wanted her to know it or if her presence was just an excuse for them to reminisce.

"Old J.W. caught on fast," Grove Miller said. "He sold two more lots on each side of the DeVoss place, but them folks never turned out too good. J.W. wouldn't talk about sellin any more land for summer places, after that. And he had it fixed in his will, they say, so's the farm can't be broke up into sections."

"Yeah, that's what they say J.W. done," the storekeeper nodded. "He caught on to them other kinds of summer people quicker'n anybody else, and acted accordingly."

Anna wondered what had disturbed J.W. Webber about the people who had bought the other lots, but she did not ask. It could have been, she thought, that they could not measure up to the DeVoss family. She bought a pound of fresh butter, eggs, coffee, and milk and drove back to the cabin. She was surprised to discover how relaxed she was. Even talking to two old men had quelled some of her loneliness.

Chapter III

Anna had stopped in Winston-Salem on her way back from the airport long enough to purchase a small portable radio. She hooked it up beside her bed and fiddled with the tuning knobs until she found an f.m. station broadcasting soft music with little chatter, out of Charlotte. She tuned it low enough to create a tranquil background of music which did not drown out the sound of Butterfly Falls. She finished unpacking, placing a towel-wrapped photograph of Pete in the bottom of the dresser drawer, under her underclothing. She had not looked at it in more than a year and dreaded experimenting with her reaction to it. When she had finished, she stood near the bed looking about her, wondering what to do with herself next. She felt entirely alone in a world of forest that reached to the farthest edges of the world. But at the moment she was not lonely. She had a feeling of visiting with herself in privacy so that she could think clearly, a time when she could pick her own mind in an effort to determine where she would go from here. Now that she had helped bury Pete, now that she knew beyond doubt that he was really dead—

gone forever (of course she did not know it at all, inside her flesh, inside her heart)—now that she had confronted the evidence, though circumstantial, the ceremony of a military farewell, had received the folded flag, she could not play her sad waiting game much longer and still be honest with herself. There was really no one to wait for. She had to move forward in some direction or suffocate.

She flung herself backward onto the bed and stared at the knotty-pine ceiling. She had not woven a winding sheet by day and unraveled it by night to put off impatient suitors. She was no Penelope. She had gone to school and had made herself useful to herself and to society as a social worker. And she had thwarted her potential suitors by flashing her wedding ring for most of the six years waiting. Even the chauvinist who had brought her news that Pete was missing in action had managed to touch her intimately while she wept briefly in his arms. But he had been dismissed, as were the others who had come after him. She had lain awake many nights alone and lonely aching for Pete. She dismissed thoughts of others.

"Anna! Anna! You've got to face the facts, damn it," Joe Suggs, Pete's wingman, had argued. "I saw it. I flew over the spot at five hundred feet three times, with those gooks shooting whole junkyards at me. There was no parachute. His ship did not burn, but it tore all to hell. Pancaked across a paddy and plunged into some woods. He *couldn't* have survived. No way! He could not! Accept that fact, baby."

But why could he not have survived? Miracles happen. Even the remains beneath his cross in Arlington might be, could possibly be someone else.

She shook her head, then closed her eyes, relaxing. She listened to the soft rendition of "Star Dust," violins and saxophones predominating. She tried to put everything out of her mind for the moment except the music, and succeeded. Soon she was asleep, fully dressed, her feet on the floor.

She awakened an hour later rested and restless. She glanced at her watch. It was a few minutes of four, and the splotches of sunlight amid the trees outside her window seemed to promise a day that would last another week. She went into the kitchen area of the cabin and found the liquor cache in an overhead cabinet. Mixing herself a gin and tonic, she returned to the bedroom and sat down in the rocker, sipping the bittersweet drink. She was thirsty, and the drink tasted good. She rocked a few inches each way while she stared at the photograph of Dr. DeVoss and his wife in their wedding garments, above the bed. Dr. DeVoss appeared to have been in his mid-twenties. He stared straight at her, a solemn grimace warping his wide mouth, but there was a twinkle in his eyes as he tried to present a bearing distinguished enough to suit posterity. If his hair had been crewcut instead of pompadoured, she thought, if he had on a uniform or jumpsuit—

A slight alcoholic haze settled across her mind, relaxing her. She stared at the picture, then smiled and winked. She could have sworn the tension around the mouth of the man in the photograph relaxed ever so slightly and that Pete DeVoss's mouth came through. She placed her drink on the floor and crossed the room to the dresser. Opening the bottom drawer, she groped beneath her clothing and found the photograph of Pete, removing it. She unwrapped it slowly, dropped the towel back into the drawer, and with the glass-covered face pressed against her breasts, she returned to the rocker.

She sat back down, took a long drink, set her glass back on the floor, then tilted the frame until she was once more face to face with her husband. Pete DeVoss grinned at her, a sandy Clark Gable mustache paralleling his thin upper lip. His chin was square and stubborn, his eyes bluer than a Carolina October sky, and his nose, high and sharp enough to cut a path through a squad of linemen and linebackers. His sandy hair stood straight up, about an inch long. ("Who gives a crap about how it looks? I got to get a helmet on over it.") Pete DeVoss had never known a country filled with his peers wearing long hair, Fu Manchu mustaches, and long sideburns. He had bowed out before the style reached the bank vice-presidents and insur-

ance salesmen. Besides, he had been gung ho military—the Spartan, the Roman centurion, specifically, the Navy attack pilot wearing his Skyhawk
like a sword and shield. Anna felt a sudden ache
in her chest. Her eyes moistened and she inhaled
deeply, preparing herself for a sob, but nothing
happened. The ache about her heart could not
even be absorbed. It remained like a cold, heavy
rock while she breathed rapidly. Then it began to
conceal its presence, leaving a vacuum.

Holding the photograph to her bosom, she lay
back, rocking slowly, remembering Pete DeVoss.

She had worked that summer at Virginia Beach
as a waitress in a family restaurant specializing in
seafood. Her parents would not hear of her working at the beach under any other circumstances.
Virginia Beach was buzzing with potential evil, and
the devil "could trap the soul and virtue of a seventeen-year-old in a split second." Yes, she could go
if she roomed with Sally Whitelaw. They had
known Sally all her life. Her father was a deacon,
she was a good girl, and being older than Anna,
Sally could guide her. What Anna's parents did not
suspect was that Sally was a "fast" girl. But this did
not bother Anna. She liked Sally for herself and
had no intentions of following her example.

It was inevitable that Sally would choose a job
as a waitress in a beer lounge. Anna wondered if it
were also inevitable that she agreed to work for
Sally one evening out of all time, when Sally was ill.

It had happened. Anna had not dared work there more than once for fear her parents would learn of it and take her back home. Pete had told her later that it was the first time he had ever visited that place and would probably have been his last.

The Jet Pilot Lounge was a busy place, frequented mostly by pilots from nearby Oceana Navy Air Base. At first Anna (wearing a long, sunburned ponytail and a short green uniform) had been shocked by the uninhibited language and brazen propositions the pilots had bombarded her with whenever she served them or passed close to their tables. But after the first hour, she relaxed, realizing that most of them were kidding and did not expect her to take them up on their offers. She was beginning to enjoy her work as her apron pockets filled up with bills, many of them fives and tens, and she envied Sally her lucrative job night after night.

Around midnight the crowd had begun to thin out, the next day being a flying day. Anna was standing near an empty booth staring out at Atlantic Avenue, where a sailor was talking to a girl in white shorts, when someone came up behind her, stood close, and kissed her on top of the head. She gasped, went rigid, and whirled, staring up into Pete DeVoss's grinning face.

"I've been watching you," he said softly. "I'd love to make out with you."

Her mouth dropped open, and she stared at him in embarrassment. While she was still motionless, before she could react further, could even think, could do anything but stare into his laughing blue eyes, he leaned forward and kissed her, barely touching her lips. "Good night, sweet baby," he grinned. "I'll see *you* later."

He had turned and walked casually toward the door, his cap on at a jaunty angle. And as she watched him go, staring at his broad shoulders, narrow waist, and the tight muscular shifting of his buttocks, she felt a warm glow deep inside, a fear and an excitement.

The next evening he appeared at the restaurant where she worked and sat alone at a back table. Sally had directed him there, Anna learned later. He could not have been more courteous. In fact, he was almost formal, he was so polite, and gave the impression he had never set eyes on her before in his life. But he could not conceal the merry twinkle in his eyes, indicating how much he enjoyed the little game he played. She was so nervous around him at first, her fingers were all thumbs. She dropped the bread basket into his salad and almost spilled coffee in his lap. But by the time he had drunk his second cup of coffee, he had put her at ease, and she was disappointed when he left without saying more than a casual "Good night," although he did leave a ten dollar tip.

But when he returned on Thursday evening to eat alone, Anna relaxed. She knew he was playing with her, and she decided to wait him out. Anna had never dated anyone alone other than a school-mate, mainly because her dates had to pass her parents' approval, and the prospect of going out with a Navy pilot somewhat older than she both terrified her and burned inside her with excitement. That night he walked her back to her apartment, taking a roundabout stroll beneath a fishing pier, and he kissed her. There was nothing passionate about it—a brief, sweet kiss of affection which had thrilled but had hardly aroused her. She wondered as they walked to her apartment, hand in hand as she had walked with her high school dates, if his behavior on Tuesday night might have been a bluff to conceal the modesty and shyness that seemed to be a part of his personality. It was only later that she realized there was nothing shy about him and that his caution had been a well-planned strategy, his moves coordinated to win her trust and affection quickly yet completely. He had learned from Sally who she was, what her background was, and he had courted her accordingly. She understood what he was up to without rationalizing about it, and it put her on guard at first. But realizing the compliment he was paying her, a young seventeen, when he could have swept any of fifty girls off their feet, including Sally, she accepted his old-fashioned courtship without shame.

Things happened fast after the walk on the beach. He saw her every night for a week, joining her in passionate embraces yet never going too far. Then he was gone for a week, on a flight to the west coast, and her world became empty and sterile. When he returned, they eloped in Pete's Porsche and were married in Charleston, South Carolina. They honeymooned in the upstairs bedroom of an old mansion owned by Pete's division commander—in the same room his great-grandmother had spent her honeymoon at sixteen, with her groom, a Confederate colonel in his late forties. When Anna was not with Pete, she could see Fort Sumter Island from her bedroom window.

Anna had approached the great climax of her life with foreboding. But Pete was so experienced and so considerate, she had no problem at all. He continued to court her, even after two days of marriage, as though they were teenage lovers with the whole world and time before them. But their marriage together was to be brief, although they did not know it at the time.

She was amazed when the honeymoon ended, so amazed and so happy that her parents had hardly crossed her mind during their week in Charleston. But when it ended, she began to worry, dreading to return to Virginia Beach and her confrontation with them. Pete found a nice apartment near the beach, and Sally solved her problem by reporting her marriage to her parents. They were so shocked and hurt at her betrayal, they would not call her or come about her until after Pete had left for Vietnam. They finally accepted her marriage enough to visit her. Although her mother had never completely forgiven her, she was relieved that God had at least been notified of the union when Anna and Pete were married in a Christian chapel, even if it had been Episcopalian, and a lateral branch of Protestantism.

The six months that had followed their honeymoon had been good, a lifetime of marriage, as much of a lifetime as she would ever have with Lieutenant Pete DeVoss. They had flown to Jacksonville and visited for three days with his parents, who were friendly enough in a formal way, as they had tried to adjust to the idea of a seventeen-year-old daughter-in-law.

It was at the parties with Pete's fellow officers and their wives that Anna got to know what he was like outside his professional life. Pete was respected as a superior pilot, but he brought none of that to the parties with him. His fellow officers, dressed in sports clothes, looked more like clerks in a shoe store on a holiday than attack pilots, and Anna found that to be a strange contradiction. She had expected to find them all like Pete, who looked the part he lived. Rarely did the pilots talk flying when drinking. Anna decided that was because the parties were their main escape from the threat of instant death that hovered over the Navy pilot more than any other combat man when not at war.

Pete, thoroughly intoxicated on Martinis made of Beefeater's gin or Oso Negro, was usually the center of what was going on at a party, regardless of where it was taking place. He was boisterous, a bit too loud at times, but always friendly. He loved his comrades, most of them, and he loved parties.

Once after he had been unusually loud telling a joke, Anna had found Pete in one of the dark bedrooms staring out a window at the night sky. She had switched on the light before she knew he was there. When he whirled, she saw tears in his eyes. She took him into her arms and he wept softly for a few minutes, then stopped abruptly as though a fuse had blown and was his old, carefree self again. But he told her later in bed that a friend that he had gone through flight training with had creamed into a Colorado mountain the day before, and he had just learned of it that night. There were other times when he would cry out in his sleep or wake up trembling, and she would hold him close, stroking his back until he relaxed, often going back to sleep in that position.

The friendship between the military couples was wonderful. The older wives were especially so-licitous of Anna because of her age, and the pilots, learning of her squeamishness about obscenity, teased her a great deal at first. But it was the military politics that made her sick. For one thing, the "ring knockers," graduates of Annapolis, were promoted first, assisted by golf games with commanding officers and dutiful wives kowtowing to superiors' wives—(superior in that their husbands were officers of rank and command.) Anna drew the line there, absolutely, refusing to kiss any hausfrau's rear because her husband had position. Pete backed her. He was a graduate of Georgia Tech and resented the unwritten laws of promotion and the pecking order among wives. The wife of the C.O., of course, was the chief hen, who used the under-ranking wives at her whim. Anna and a few other wives resisted and were ostracized for it, but could not have cared less.

Once when the squadron had gone on a week of sea maneuvers off Puerto Rico, the commanding officer's wife had thought up the hilarious project of supplying each husband with a D-cup brassiere stuffed with cotton, for a head rest in his plane. Anna had thought the idea was stupid and had refused to cooperate. Soon after the planes had landed at Oceana Naval Base, his skipper had called Pete into his office and started to chew him out because of Anna's behavior.

After three sentences, Pete interrupted. "You mean, sir, you ordered me in here to dress me down because my wife refused to supply me with a head rest made from a stuffed brassiere?" Pete asked politely.

"Dammit, it's not that simple, Lieutenant De-Voss," the C.O. said. "We are a close organization, and our wives—"

"My wife, sir, is not in the Navy," Pete said firmly. "My wife does not do anything she does not want to do, where the Navy is concerned. Your wife outweighs my wife, sir, but she does not out-rank her."

The officer had reddened. "Are you defying me, Lieutenant?"

"No sir! I am a pilot. I'd follow you to hell and you know it—or fly there alone if you ordered me to. But stuffed brassieres for military head rests—" He stopped, feigning a loss for words.

"It was just a bit of wifely humor," his C.O. argued. "I resent the fact that you—"

"Sir," Pete had said quietly, "I have a family acquaintance in the Pentagon. If you like, I'll call or write and get the Pentagon's opinion concerning the practicality of stuffed brassieres for head rests in Skyhawks and Intruders."

The officer turned white, his flexing fingers breaking the pencil in his hands. "Lieutenant, you are dismissed!" he said quietly. Pete had saluted, he had told Anna later, done a smart about-face, and followed his grin out of the skipper's office. Anna laughed hilariously when told of the event.

It was this self-respect and individuality he was able to retain in a military world that increased Anna's respect for him, and increased pride in the husband she had chosen. She realized early that he had little ambition for rank, as such. It was flying he was interested in, and the salary that went with it. He could live better with a higher rank. He had elaborate plans for buying a farm someday in Watauga County and returning there to raise cattle, horses, and children. He wanted four children, he told her, two boys and two girls. He wanted to become a sturdy old grandfather to sixteen grandchildren and tell them tales of the days when he rode his thundering steed across the sky—always recounted with a grin, but she understood how very serious he was.

She remembered now, in a flash, the day she stood on an apron at Oceana Naval Base and held him in her arms, kissing him for the last time. She watched him, heavy with gear, waddle toward the humpbacked little Skyhawk, his orange jumpsuit and helmet giving him the appearance of a creature from outer space. A few minutes later she blinked as she stared at the hole in the sky where his plane had disappeared. And that was the end.

Anna sighed, stood up, and carried the photograph back to the dresser, placing it at an angle so she could see it from her bed. Lieutenant Commander Pete DeVoss would never know one child, let alone sixteen grandchildren. Instead of a stuffed brassiere, the spinning earth had become his head rest.

Chapter IV

After three days at the cabin, Anna could tell neither the day of the week nor the date, unless she stopped to think about it—that is, the day of the week. As for the date, she knew it was early June, and that was enough. Twice, she did not bother to put her watch back on after a shower. The hands continued to carry out their appointed function. Blossoms had begun to fade and drop from the rhododendron thicket, but a flame azalea she found near Butterfly Falls lit up the oak and pine thicket around it with orange brilliance. She knew what it was because she had found a paperback book on mountain wildflowers in one of the bookcases in the cabin and carried it with her into the forest when she became restless and felt like taking a hike. It got to be a mild adventure with her, finding plants and flowers she had never seen before and identifying them. She found a clump of lady's-slippers with three wilting blossoms which had lost their pink hue. She picked some brilliant fire-pink, sweet shrub (aromatic as an exotic perfume), and black-eyed Susans and mixed them with the polished green leaves she plucked from a carpet of galax, making a centerpiece for the lamp stand in the center of the lazy-Susan table. She was surprised to find black-eyed Susans blooming so early. Another time she came upon a dwarf magnolia tree in full bloom in the middle of the forest and was puzzled until she looked it up and saw that it was a mountain cousin of the "southern-belle" lawn variety, called Fraser Magnolia, named for a botanist, James Fraser, who first discovered the tree in the Appalachians.

On Friday—at least she thought it was Friday—she put on her last year's bathing suit, took a blanket from the window box, and headed for Butterfly Falls. She took along the radio. She spread the blanket on a flat area of the rock beside the pool, turned on the radio to a low murmur a bit louder than the gush of the falls, and lay down on her stomach. Ragged splotches of sunshine dappled the trees and the bank across the stream, although she lay in the shade. A morning coolness enveloped her side of the stream, but it was a comfortable cool. She turned onto her back and watched a small heart-shaped cloud as it crossed the patch of sky directly overhead.

The sun spilled over the brim of the oak and pine limbs high overhead, washing her in pools of warmth. She tugged at the leg of her trunks, the hem of which was cutting her. She squirmed to a new position, but moments later, in exasperation, she sat up, removed the narrow black bottom, then the halter, and lay back on the blanket nude, enjoying the probing warm sunlight. Several minutes later she began to wonder if the sunshine here, high in the mountains, would burn her as quickly as at the beach. But she felt free and unencumbered, naked in the middle of a forest with nothing but butterflies and birds to see her.

But suppose there really were such things as satyrs, and one of them watched from the woods. Or suppose Pan, with his goat rear, was ready to spring at her? Or suppose that there really was a Zeus and he watched her, ready to turn himself into a swan or a bull—She giggled aloud, then rolled her head to one side and stared out into the trees. She could see only the chest, shoulders, and part of his curly head with horns, and she smiled back, then tilted her head back to watch the clouds. Was it the ghost of her imagination?

She had just finished drying herself after a long shower when someone knocked with authority on the front door. She knew it was going to be a man as she crossed the cabin, fighting her arms into the faded blue robe. The tableau was repeated. She opened the door just as Jay Webber raised his freckled fist to knock again. So far as she could tell, he even had on the same jeans and shirt he had worn last time. And she certainly had on the same old dilapidated robe.

He looked her up and down, his face without expression. "Ain't you got no clothes but that, lady?" he asked solemnly.

Her first impulse was to burst out laughing. But looking at him more closely, she decided he was serious. If there was one thing she did not need, it was a smartaleck peckerwood. "Yes, what of it?" she demanded, more brusquely than she really intended.

"Oh, yes, it just occurred to me that I ought to point out a couple of places you might have trouble." He hesitated, ran his fingers through his kinky hair, looking uncertainly from her towards the woods. "Could—could I come in?"

"Surely, Mr. Webber. Do come in."

He entered and she closed the door, turned toward him. "Do you mind waiting a few minutes till I get something else on? I do feel out of uniform with nothing on but this old robe. Take a chair there." She motioned toward the chairs by the fireplace.

He nodded solemnly and sat down. She returned to her bedroom and dressed in a plaid pantsuit and sandals. When she re-entered the living area, Jay Webber was standing by the sink looking out the window. As she approached, he leaned across and raised the window sash a few inches. Immediately, Anna heard a weird barking sound out in the woods. She could not tell whether it was an animal or a bird, but she had never heard anything like it before.

"Come here a minute," he commanded softly, summoning her with a curl of a finger over his shoulder.

She approached, stood beside him. "Look there!" He pointed. "See that little reddish lump on that limb there?"

She leaned forward across the sink, staring, and her shoulder touched his. She drew back quickly. She was almost sure she could smell an astringent odor about him, not old sweat, but new, as though he had been working hard recently. The nails on his pointing hand needed cleaning. There was what looked like blue dirt beneath them.

"What is it?" she asked. "It—it looks like a little squirrel."

"It is a kind of squirrel. It's called a boomer. I've not seen one around here in years."

"Noisy little beggar," Anna laughed. "What happened to them?"

"They're about extinct in this region of the Appalachians." He turned to face her. "Soon they'll join the buffalo, elk, and the passenger pigeons. Used to be so common, they named a post office after them over near Wilkesboro. It's still there, I reckon."

"You mean there's a place called Boomer, N.C.?" She smiled. "Doesn't sound too romantic."

"There was. I reckon it serves the needs of the folks who live there." He turned away. "Dr. DeVoss had the fuse box replaced with circuit breakers about four years ago." He reached up and opened the cabinet door to the right of the sink. On the wall at the back was a metal door. He opened it and revealed double rows of switches. Each switch had a piece of kitchen equipment or an area of the house printed on a piece of tape beside it. Jay Webber placed a finger on the switch marked *stove*. "If your stove won't turn on, it will be this breaker. It cuts off from time to time. No reason I can find. Just switch it back on."

"Well, thank you. That's important to know—I suppose."

"One other thing. Your water may stop on you sometime. Would you come with me, please."

His voice sounded more like a command than a request or suggestion, and she felt like telling him to bug off, then thought better. If he could save her trouble later on, why not? He had not tried to get familiar with her, and as long as he behaved himself, he might be useful occasionally.

She followed him out of the house and walked beside him as he climbed the slope of the ridge above the cabin. The boomer had fled, along with his raucous bark, into the past. There was little undergrowth, making the climb fairly easy, although Anna could feel in her legs a pulling at muscles she did not know she had. They came upon a huge gray rock and circled it. A spring as large as a child's wading pool sparkled in the shadows beneath the edge of the boulder, the spring tail trickling off down the hill toward the brook above Butterfly Falls.

"This is the sweetest spring water you'll ever taste," Jay Webber said. Anna detected pride in his voice, as though he had dug the spring with his bare hands. "See that pipe jutting out there, about a foot from the bank, on your left?"

She braced her hands on her knees, leaned forward, and peered deep into the clear water. She could make out a section of pipe extending into the spring, about two feet down. Light refraction distorted it, causing it to appear crooked. There was a cap of screen wire over the end of it.

"On rare occasions a leaf or two will sink down and be drawn over the end of the pipe. That's your water supply, down there. It's gravity-fed. If your water should happen to stop flowing or slow to a trickle, it'll probably be because of a leaf. Just come out here and uncover the end, and you'll be okay again. But you rarely have any trouble during the summer."

"That makes sense," she said. "Yes, I can understand that." She tried to think of something else she could say to the young mountain farmer, something bright and feminine, but she could not. She considered saying something about the cattle she had seen in the pasture on the ridge, or asking him what kinds of crops he grew. She certainly knew about cattle and feed. But she rejected the idea. She did not feel like being a hypocrite with him, and she really was not interested in establishing a relationship, even a casual one. As close as he lived to her cabin, he could become a pest, and she needed to be alone for a while. But he was company.

They walked back down the ridge, mostly in silence. Once, he stopped to point to a weird little flower growing in a mulchy area beside a white rock. There was a deep bell-like throat with what looked like a single petal looped up and over, to form a canopy above its mouth, out of which projected a tapered pistil. Because of the flower's greenish hue, it was camouflaged against its own leaves.

"That's a Jack-in-the-pulpit," he said. "Some folks call it Indian turnip. The roots are edible if you can stand the taste."

"Good. If I ever get lost in the woods, I won't starve."

He turned his head and looked into her eyes with narrowed amber ones, so intently she had to look away from them, watching his mouth. "You might," he said, the trace of a smile arching his lips between mustache and beard. "They aren't that easy to find, unless you know where to look."

When they reached the front steps, he stopped and she climbed to the deck, then turned to look down at him. "Well, thanks a lot. I ought to be pretty secure now."

He braced his right hand against the trunk of a small hickory and squinted up at her, a light in his eyes she had not seen there before, something between amusement and resentment. "You're welcome, Mrs. DeVoss." He pronounced the *Mrs.* the way Henry Sparr had, and it sounded so natural she could not tell whether he was needling her or serious.

She turned away, then turned back. "I'm curious about one thing. It's not important. I just wondered."

"Yes, ma'am? What can I tell you?"

"You called Mrs. DeVoss *Maud,* and she's much older than I am. I wondered why you did that and call me *Mrs.*"

He laughed, looked down and scuffed one battered shoe against the ground, then looked up into her face, his head cocked to one side. "Well, now, I've known Maud since I was a boy. Long time ago we worked out what we'd call each other. You called me *Mr.* Webber a little while back. I figured that was how you wanted it, ma'am."

"Oh!" She stared at him. It was true. "Oh, yes. I'd forgotten. Well, thanks again."

She entered the cabin. As she was closing the door, he called her again. She thrust her head outside, past the door. "You wanted something else?"

"Not really. There is one other thing you might want to hear about."

"What is it?" She moved into the doorway, watching him climb the steps to the deck.

When he reached her, she backed to one side, allowing him to enter the house. She watched him closely, feeling insecure with him confronting her now. And that annoyed her. She did not like to feel insecure. It weakened her defenses, making her vulnerable. She was not used to that.

"Could we go into your bedroom, ma'am. Used to be where the DeVosses slept." A half smile flickered across his mouth.

She was startled. She looked from his large, freckled arms below the sleeves of his shirt toward the open bedroom door, then back at him. "Is—is it important?"

"Well, not to me, ma'am. Not really." He turned back toward the open door. "I was just thinking of you."

"Well—very well." She laughed a strained little laugh. "Let's see what it is."

He followed her into the bedroom, and when she stopped near the dresser, he crossed the floor and dropped to one knee beside the window seat.

He raised the lid. "Would you please come over here for a moment, ma'am?"

She crossed to where she could see into the shadowy interior of the box. On the end panel, nearest the bed, was what looked like an electric button, two small wires leading from it downward toward the floor.

"That's an alarm button. It rings a bell in our house. Mrs. DeVoss—Maud had me put it in two years ago, after the doctor died. She never has used it, but she said she always felt better knowing it was there." He closed the lid and stood up.

"You mean those wires reach all the way to your house?" she demanded. "Why, that's half a mile."

"No, just to the nearest electric fence, back in the woods there, a ways."

He moved toward the door, pausing to look at Pete's photograph, on the dresser. Then he crossed the living room in silence, turning at the front door.

"If you should get scared—like if a satyr threatens you—you just give me a ring. I'll come a-running."

For a few seconds she studied his head, thinking how much he himself looked like the picture of a satyr she had seen somewhere. "Thank you very much. I do feel safer. But don't stay awake for my signal. I'm not your timid kid. My husband taught me to defend myself."

He threw her a little wave of his hand that

could have meant anything and opened the door, started to close it after him.

"Hey!" she called.

He paused, looked back.

"Thanks for the information—Jay."

His kinky gold beard and mustache parted in a grin. He nodded and closed the door after him. She heard him chuckle on the deck.

Later that same day Anna was rummaging through some papers and letters in the top dresser drawer when she ran across the DeVoss membership card in the Grayhound Lodge and Country Club, "including members of the family and guests." She tossed it back, thinking no more about it until the next afternoon, which was a Saturday. Around five o'clock she became suddenly hungry for a good meal, something like steak or lobster, which she was in no mood to prepare for herself. Besides, she was tired of eating her own piddling meals of easy-fixit hamburger combinations and cold plates. She walked around the living area of the cabin looking for the telephone, intending to call the Grayhound Lodge and find out what was on the menu for the day that she would be interested in. When she remembered there was no telephone, something she had known since arriving, she sat down in a chair in the reading area and stared out the window into the woods. She felt suddenly stupid. Or did that explain her sudden lapse of memory? Was she becoming eccentric so soon, all alone here in an Appalachian forest with no one to talk with? She considered packing and heading back toward Norfolk and civilization, but immediately canceled the idea. A cool breath of mountain air billowed through the window, and she compared it, below the level of conscious consideration, with the humid steam bath of a coastal June.

She sat there so long the forest began to darken, and she realized the sun was going down behind Beech Mountain, ushering in the long, tranquil period of mountain twilight—twilight outside the forest. Here beneath the trees, darkness would come swiftly. Her stomach burbled hungrily, the sound startling her in the quiet cabin. Without conscious decision, she got to her feet and crossed to her bedroom, where she began to dress for dinner at the Grayhound Lodge, or elsewhere if she did not like the menu there.

She dressed in a white blouse and a pale blue, ankle-length skirt, as usual not bothering with makeup. It was 8:45 when she drove out of the woods and onto the Ridge Road, but there was a sky full of daylight left to spend. She swung down the spur of the ridge, crossed the river, and speeded up on the stretch of asphalt beyond. When she saw a man in coveralls by a gasoline truck parked in front of Sparr's Store, she hit the brakes and swung into the parking area, stopping close to the truck. The man whirled, then grinned at her, touching his cap visor with the tips of his fingers.

"Yes, ma'am, I know where the Grayhound Lodge is at. You jest drive on down the road there till you come to the main highway, then you turn right, and about a half a mile furder on, you can see a sign on the left and a road leading off beside it. You can't hardly miss it, less'n you was blind. Yes, ma'am, you shore are most welcome." As she drove away, Anna was smiling to herself, not in derision, but at the music of the man's dialect.

She got up to forty at times, swinging around the curves which paralleled the river. She switched on her headlights in the gloom beneath the arch of overlapping trees. Back in daylight on the highway, she found the sign indicating the turnoff to the lodge easily enough. After following another segment of the river for a quarter of a mile, she turned left across a pool-table green of a golf course, toward a mountain which reared up a short distance ahead, or at least what had once been a mountain. It was now the foundation or backdrop for scores of chalets of every shape and size, from A-frame to toadstool construction. They were scattered without pattern across the green mountainside, their order apparently determined by the shape and location of the lot on which each stood. Lights were already on in some of those lower down. Those toward the top of the mountain were washed in a wan yellow glow from the light of overhead clouds still fingered by rays of the sinking sun, below the mountain horizon.

The road swung left off the golf course at a small sentinel kiosk, which was empty. A hundred yards farther along the base of the mountain, Grayhound Lodge sprawled along the edge of the golf course, a rambling structure built of native stone and rough, brown-stained timber. A small red flag with a black Grayhound's head on it fluttered from a staff above the cedar shake roof.

The receptionist, a comely lady in her forties, sat behind a small service window in the wall, to the right of the entrance hallway, several coat racks in the room behind her. She watched Anna curiously as she entered and approached her.

"Good evening," Anna greeted. She presented the DeVoss membership card.

The woman glanced at it, then smiled brightly. "Oh, yes, the DeVoss family. And you are—"

"I'm the daughter-in-law. I'm—was Pete's wife."

The woman's face lost its smile. "Yes, Pete! We were terribly sorry to hear about him. He was well liked." Then the smile returned. "I'm Betty. I'm pleased to meet you, Mrs. DeVoss." She paused. "Were you planning to have dinner?"

"I wanted to, if possible," she said. "I'm famished."

"Did—did you have a reservation?"

"No. You see, there's no phone at the DeVoss cabin, and I decided on the spur of the moment to come."

"I remember, the DeVoss family never had a telephone." The receptionist looked serious for a moment. "Let me see." She picked up the phone and dialed three numbers, spoke briefly to someone in the dining room.

Placing the phone back, she smiled. "No problem tonight, fortunately. There had been a cancellation. You just go into the dining room and George will seat you."

"Thank you." Anna smiled and turned quickly away, making her way down the hallway before some special catastrophe could cheat her of the dinner she craved so much.

She sat at a table for two in the far corner of the dim-lit dining room. A third of the tables were empty, but they all had RESERVED cards on them. The others were filled with patrons, from two to eight in the party. Several diners had looked at her curiously as she followed the head waiter alone across the floor. Three tables away, to her right, two men and a woman dined, the husband or date of the woman, obviously, with his back to Anna. She caught the extra man watching her two or three times, and once she was sure he had said something about her to the woman, who looked Anna's way. He was a dark executive type, around thirty-five, dressed in a white dinner jacket.

She forgot her neighbors when her waiter approached and handed her a wine list. "I'm not in the mood for wine," she told him. "Could I have a cocktail of some kind?"

"Do you have a locker, ma'am?" The waiter leaned stiffly toward her. "I mean, in this state, ma'am, they don't have open bars yet. You have to furnish your own liquor."

"Yes, I see," Anna nodded. "I had forgotten. I'm on the DeVoss card. I'm sure the DeVosses must have a locker."

"I'll check, ma'am." He bowed slightly and turned away, almost performing an about-face, returning to the bar, out of sight beyond the other end of the dining room. In a few minutes he was back. "Yes, there is a DeVoss locker, ma'am." He smiled, extending a small slip of paper with printing on it, along with a pen. "You'll have to sign this. It gives the bartender permission to open the locker, if you don't mind." Then he added, "Of course, if you'd rather do it yourself—"

"That's fine." She tried to read the print on the slip, but the candlelight was too dim. She gave up and signed it, handing it back to the waiter. "I'd like something light, please," she said. "Like a whiskey sour."

"Very good. A whiskey sour, ma'am."

The salad was delicious, the baked potato smothered in sour cream was fattening but worth every calorie, and the prime rib, medium rare, was exactly what she had needed. Anna ate slowly, feeling her hunger gradually dwindle and disappear. It was 10:30 before she had finished the meal. She suspected without making an issue of it that she was prolonging her visit here among people she could relate to, delaying her return to the lonely cabin. Yet she had no desire to meet any of the members of the lodge—not tonight anyway. Her coffee and dessert—cheese cake two inches thick—lasted another half-hour.

When the waiter brought Anna her check, she asked if she might visit the bar for a while and pay for the meal and drink at the same time. He assured her she could and left with the check, heading back toward the bar. She left a tip and followed the waiter. She felt content and was satisfied with the service.

The tables in the narrow little lounge were all filled, but the bar stools were empty except for the one at the near end, occupied by a bald man in a dark suit, who looked as though he might be some kind of manager. Anna made her way down the narrow passage among the tables, aware of several curious glances from the summer people, who probably knew each other, and selected the stool on the far end of the bar from the other occupant.

The bartender, a heavy, sandy-haired young man in a red livery jacket, came over to where she sat. His white jowls jiggled in rhythm to the shaker in his hands. "Evening, Mrs. Devoss." He smiled, his teeth as broad as white grains of corn. "I'm Tony. What could I serve you?"

"I'd like a brandy, Tony, if we have any in the locker."

He frowned, his round face going sad. "I'm afraid there's no brandy of any kind in your locker, ma'am. Perhaps I could find a remnant someone left—"

"Was—is there any Jack Daniels?"

His face brightened like the full moon appearing from behind a cloud. "Yes, ma'am. There's at least half a fifth. Black label."

"Then give me Jack Daniels and branch water, Tony. Okay?"

"Okay, ma'am. Coming right up."

Anna sipped at her drink and studied the bottles on the shelves back of the bar. She tried to see how many labels she could read without squinting. She did not pay any attention to the man who sat down on the second stool away until he spoke to her.

"All alone tonight," he said or asked, she could not tell which.

She lowered the glass and turned to look at him. It was the same man she had noticed in the dining room. Italian derivative, she thought, or something like that. Maybe central Europe ancestors, not that it mattered in the melting pot that was America. His nose was Romanesque, projecting from between heavy brows as thick as hedge rows. He would have had a cold, commanding face had it not been for his eyes. They were brown and gentle as a beagle pup's, she thought. Anna flashed him a stiff smile. "Just me and Harvey, here." She embraced a huge, invisible figure on the stool to her left.

For a moment, he stared quizzically at her. Then he grinned. "It was a rather naive gambit, wasn't it?"

"I thought so," Anna replied, and took another sip of her drink.

Tony approached, polishing a glass and smiling. "Mrs. DeVoss, this is Mr. Grunwald," he said.

Anna cut at the bartender with a narrow look. She could have kicked his legs from beneath him.

"How do you do, Mrs. DeVoss," the man said.

"As Tony gratuitously stated, I am Mrs. DeVoss."

He looked at her in puzzlement. Then he leaned toward her. "I'm a direct man, Mrs. DeVoss. Let me explain. I'm not trying to pick you up. This is not some big city bar. We are a rather close group here. About everyone knows everyone else. I realized you were a stranger and thought I'd drop by the bar and say *howdy*."

Anna set her glass down and turned farther toward him. "I'm sorry. I guess it's my old defense mechanism. I didn't particularly feel like conversation tonight, and I really was trying to discourage you."

"I understand how you feel," he nodded. His

voice was deep and resonant. Tony brought him a drink and he took it, sipped. "I wondered about the *Mrs.*, though, since you wear no rings."

Anna resented the implied question but let it pass. "I'm a widow," she said.

"Oh, I'm sorry." He stared into his glass a moment, then said, "You going to be around here long?"

"I have no idea."

"I'm unattached, myself," Mark Grunwald stated. "Could I call you sometime?"

"Would you believe I don't have a telephone where I'm staying?" She smiled an especially sweet smile.

He studied her, his brown eyes sadder than ever. "No, I wouldn't." he said. "That would be hard to believe." He got up and left the bar, leaving his drink almost untouched.

Anna felt a little bit of a bitch in a way, although she was pleased too. And she had told him the truth about the telephone. Her rejection could not have been more civilized or more effective.

Pete would chuckle when she told him—She cut the thought short, startled. She had not thought about Pete in that way in a long time. She wondered whether she was too intoxicated to drive back to the cabin.

Chapter V

Around eleven on Sunday morning, Anna left the cabin, intending to cruise around and see a few of the tourist attractions in the area. Thunder clouds sputtered and rumbled around the horizon, especially to the west, although the sky overhead was clear, except for haycock clouds tumbling east and switching the sunlight off and on. She drove west (or was it southwest?) past the turnoff to Gray-hound Lodge, climbing the long grade into Avery County. Grandfather Mountain jutted skyward, across the valley to her left, its rocky Scot profile etched against the sky. She could make out the mile-high bridge swinging between what she took to be the lip and chin and decided she would drive up there for a look-see. In the beautiful little vacation village of Linville a man in new overalls leaning against the wall of a closed service station told her she could take U.S. 221 towards Blowing Rock, drive about two and a half miles, and come to the ticket gate and roadway leading to the top of Grandfather, on her left.

But by the time she climbed the slope of the Blue Ridge and reached the gate, she had changed her mind and continued along the winding little highway. A short distance beyond, she came to a construction area. Engineers were in the process of building the last link of the Blue Ridge Parkway along the eastern flank of Grandfather, a link which had waited for almost fifty years. But today, Sunday, everything was quiet. On impulse, Anna turned right onto the southern end of the Parkway. For a hundred yards or so she drove cautiously over the rough roadbed, newly constructed, until she came to the old paved road. Then she continued at the posted speed of 45.

The cool mountain air stirred her short hair, cooling her face and arms, and the sun was a warm infrared bulb just above her head. Wildflowers flanked the right-of-way in gaudy profusion, oxeye daisies, queen Anne's lace, and clumps of what looked to her like goldenrod. Occasionally, she passed grassy pastures and bordering meadows filled with such a variety of flowers it was hard to distinguish one of them from another.

Suddenly, bone-gray rail fences lined the Parkway and funneled off into a side road to the left. A sign indicated that Linville Falls Camp Ground and Linville Falls were in that direction. With no traffic to interfere, she made an impulsive turn to the left on squealing tires. She passed the campground on the right and about a mile farther came to a dead end in a parking area. Several vehicles were already parked there—an orange Volkswagen bug, two camping vans, a pickup camper from Canada, a pickup, several American gas guzzlers, and a ranger's car. A family of six children and their parents was eating lunch out of the back of the green Ford pickup, carefully disposing of their refuse in a large paper bag a little girl had assumed custody of. The vehicle carried an Oregon license plate.

Anna parked and walked toward the footbridge which spanned the rush of Linville River at that point. She wondered if the stream was polluted or just murky from recent rains. A young ranger stood on the bridge, his hands braced on the railing, and stared down into the stream. He was so damned good looking in his uniform, so boyishly masculine, Anna felt a sudden response deep inside and was startled by it. She stopped near him.

"Hi!" she said.

He was already smiling as he turned his head, and she was aware, resenting the fact, that she was probably only the latest of many pretty women who had approached him that day. He was a Boy Scout who had been touched by his fairy godmother's wand and turned into a ranger in a flash.

"How far do you have to walk to reach the falls?" she asked.

The ranger touched the brim of his hat. "All the way, lady," he said solemnly. Then he laughed. "I'm sorry. I've been asked that five times since I've been standing here on this bridge. I've been saving that answer for someone special."

"Why didn't you save it till next season?" Anna smiled, feeling a bit put down and stupid because his answer had bothered her.

"I apologize, really. It's a half mile walk, maybe." His eyes flickered toward her legs, below her red, white, and blue striped skirt and back to her face so fast she hardly caught the movement. "You'll enjoy it. Families with small children walk it all the time. It's a beautiful trail. Rough in places, though. Watch your step."

"Thank you. You've probably talked me into walking my legs off, but here goes."

"Ma'am," he said, "that would be a pity."

His voice was so solemn, Anna had to laugh. "Aw, go—catch a crippled fish!" she retorted, and passed him. Somehow, she felt better, not so alone as before. She glanced at the light ring of flesh around her finger where her engagement and wedding rings had been. It was beginning to darken and disappear.

It was indeed a pleasant walk, at least the first three-fourths of it, along a trail wide enough for a truck. Most of the trees were of medium height and of such a variety Anna could not begin to identify more than the most common ones, such as oak and pine. But here and there among them, giant oaks, white pines, and poplars towered toward the sky, along with another kind she believed to be hemlock, taller than the cedars, with a mass of branches curving downward and out, supporting green fronds which turned the day into twilight beneath them. Tall enough for a mast on Noah's ark, she thought. They were the remnants of a virgin forest, she guessed, and what a sad remainder. The forest here in pioneer days must have been something to behold. Shaggy carpets of fern grew on either side of the wide trail, nice gardens for the wee folk Pete had told her about. There was a scattering of wild-flowers, visited tentatively by a few yellow and black butterflies.

About two-thirds of the way to the falls, the trail curled to the right, spreading into a small clearing in which a water fountain and a comfort station were located. Dropping away to the left, almost in-cidentally, a narrow, damp, and rocky foot trail etched its way along the slope of the ridge, leading gradually downward toward an ever-increasing roar of water. Here, the air was heavy with a cool dampness, as though Anna walked the corridor of a cave. Narrow stone steps led downward to a chaos of stone split asunder by roaring water.

Upstream, a segment of Linville Falls spilled over a low stone bluff in twin fans of foaming water, an island of rock between them, and filled a quiet pool some fifty feet across. From there, the stream funneled into a narrow flume cut through bleached, stratified stone—she could see the layers clearly—and circled to the right, falling swiftly in a white skein of foam and water. It made another turn to the left, completing the S-conformation, to disappear beneath the lip of a massive peninsula thrust out above it toward the cliff on her right. From beyond the last turn, Anna could hear a deeper roar as the water churned downward through the trough of Linville Gorge, the right hand cliff of which towered above the 3,000 foot elevation where she stood (a plaque by the stone steps had indicated the altitude). Linville Gorge, Pete had once told her, was the most rugged slice of wilderness left in eastern America. He had back-packed in there once and felt as though he had gone backward two hundred years.

Ten or twelve tourists, from an old couple to toddling babes, were working their way about the rocky platform above the rapids like ants on bread crumbs, doing tourist things like taking pictures, talking, and risking their lives by leaning out too far above the water. A young woman in green shorts was telling the old lady that a nine-year-old boy had fallen into the rapids a few months back and his body had not been found for several days. While she was talking, the five-year-old boy, whose hand she had just released, leaned far out over the stream to get a better look. Bracing her hands against the same parapet, Anna leaned out and stared downward into the moiling water. She shuddered. She tried to imagine the terror of the little boy as he shot downward, hurled from rock wall to rock wall until he lost consciousness. It was beyond her imagination. A whirling green landscape, seen through a plane's canopy, came rushing at her, and she covered her eyes, wiping it out.

When Anna returned to the parking area and was about to get into her car, she saw the ranger she had encountered earlier. He was talking with a big woman with dyed red hair, but excused himself when he saw Anna and hurried toward her, smiling brightly.

"How did you like it?" He stood with feet apart, hands clasped behind him, like a soldier at ease.

"It really was a beautiful walk," she said. "And the falls are really—terrifying and beautiful."

He looked thoughtful. "I've never heard them described like that before. But I know what you mean. You're from Virginia, I see."

Anna smiled her tight defensive smile. "At least my car is, isn't it?"

"Come on, now," the ranger laughed. "I told you I was sorry. After all, I did save my smart comment especially for you."

"I was kidding. Yes, I'm from Norfolk." She slammed the door and started the engine. "Where does the name *Linville* come from?"

"A man named Linville and his son were attacked and left for dead by local Indians back around 1776. They survived by eating blackberries and holding onto an old nag the Indians had left behind."

Anna frowned and shuddered. "What a way to become immortal!"

He laughed. "Where are you staying? Close by?"

She looked upward into his tilted face. "Watauga County," she stated. She slipped into reverse.

His face became a mask of seriousness. "Well, have a good day, ma'am." He touched the brim of his hat. "You ought to try the Mineral Museum and Crabtree Falls, farther south."

"Thank you, but some other day." She backed out and left him staring after her, the rearview mirror catching the puzzled frown on his handsome face. Anna laughed softly, feeling suddenly good.

The following Monday night was so cool, Anna built a small fire in the fireplace, from wood she had found piled behind the cabin, and sat on the black bearskin rug before it, with the lights out, sipping brandy and listening to soft music from the radio. She wore only a thin mint-colored shortie gown and her panties, but she was quite comfortable near the fire. She was fascinated by the patterns forming and shifting in the flames and stared at them a long time, her mind in neutral, only her senses of sight, taste, and sound emphasized (her sense of touch, too, of course, her buttocks and feet in contact with the hairy rug)—hearing, because the cabin and the forest around it were absolutely quiet, except for the soft whisper and crackle of the flames and the music: taste, the bite of her drink; sight, the flames. She might have been on a small island isolated from the planet earth, so far as her senses were concerned. Once she tugged at the hem of her gown, glancing toward the slate-black surface of a window, then forgot the gesture.

She thought of the young ranger (had he been a park or a forest ranger?) and laughed in a sudden swell of merriment that stopped abruptly. She was surprised at the loudness of her voice in the almost silent cabin, and it startled her momentarily. But she continued to smile at the flickering flames. She thought of Mark Grunwald, wearing coat and tie— she could not imagine him in work clothes—and in a brief flash she remembered Jay Webber in his country garb leaning with his hand braced against a tree in the yard, squinting up at her on the deck. This memory was followed by a rapid train of men she had known casually and had looked at more than twice in the last two years, their faces flashing by her as their heads rode an invisible assembly belt out of the darkness and back into darkness: a male colleague back in Norfolk, the manager of the club she sometimes frequented, her sister's husband, one of Pete's old friends who dropped by her apartment occasionally, the young druggist who dispensed her pills, a state congressman who lived on her hall—on and on until they dwindled into blank faces like flesh-colored balloons.

Her situation was ideal for a romantic interlude here tonight—the sequestered cabin, good brandy, music, a fire in the fireplace, a pretty woman (she knew she was pretty). Then why was she so damned content, so satisfied with herself under those conditions, all alone? She *was* content. She wore a cloak of tranquility she had not known for a long time. She was completely content to sit there sipping brandy, listening, and watching the fire. At the moment, she did not want to be with anyone else or to be anywhere else. Maybe being alone so much was getting to be an unchangeable routine. Maybe these mountains were working a spell on her. Then she thought of the handsome ranger and of Mark Grunwald, and she swallowed a bitter little lump that formed in her throat.

When the fire died down to embers, she returned to her bedroom and switched on the light. For an instant she stared at the face of the strange young man who watched her from the photograph frame on her dresser. Where had she known him before, her groggy mind asked.

After preparing to retire, she raised the window beside her bed as high as it would go, removed her gown, and slept in a cocoon of warmth beneath a blanket and the patchwork quilt, with summer colors in its design.

Thursday was more like April than June, the sky a Duke University blue, almost violet. The slight stirring of a breeze was refreshingly cool when Anna encountered it in the sunshine, almost chilly when it caressed her in the shade. For breakfast, she fried country sausage spiced with red pepper and ate the patties between canned biscuits, drinking coffee so hot it almost scorched her tongue. While she was eating, it occurred to her that she ought to run over and visit Mrs. Webber. The old lady might expect it, and she did not want to seem like a cityfied snob, even if they had never met. Besides, the walk would do her good.

She dressed in blue jeans and a khaki sleeveless shirt, then selected a putter from the golf bag she had found in a storage closet. The club was an afterthought. Most country folk, she knew, had one or more dogs, and she did not want to look stupid by backing against a tree with her hands up in surrender while some asinine dog barked at her. She had no use for the putter except as a weapon. Long ago, she had become convinced that no one honestly liked T.S. Eliot, Scotch whiskey, or golf. Pete had once announced that he could not understand how a big, mature man could swing one time at a little white ball and then have to walk or ride a mile before he got to hit it again.

Anna strolled along the Ridge Road looking about her. Far to the west and north, a rim of blue-green hills spanned an arc of Holy Rood Valley. Beyond them were higher, bluer mountains, and somewhere beyond them, she knew, lay Tennessee. The ridge sloped off at first gradually to the north, then more steeply, ending in a hedge of forest she assumed paralleled Watauga River. Farther downstream, the trees puddled into a circular woods, through whose foliage she could discern a cleared space and what looked like the dark roof of a large house. Closer to her, cattle grazed, the cows with udders so small she knew they were for beef. In the near distance, two horses grazed, one red and the other a darker brown. They looked like Tennessee walkers, but they were so far away, she could not be sure.

The Webber farmhouse was an elongated structure, one end nestled into the slope with a stone foundation, the other end projecting out over the incline, below which had been built what looked like a stone basement, except most of it was above ground. The uphill section of the farmhouse was two stories high and looked to be decades older than the downhill addition. Beyond the house, Anna could see a barn and several other outbuildings. She gripped the putter a bit more firmly as she approached, but the beautiful Irish setter that appeared from around the house trotted toward her with tongue lolling and tail wagging. He sniffed at Anna's knees, and she stopped to ruffle the hair of his head.

When Anna was within fifty feet of the steps, which climbed the slope toward the front door, she stopped. A white hen came into view around the end of the house, clucking and strutting, followed by a dozen yellow "biddies." The last chicks were followed immediately by a girl of ten with long red hair, who would squat to inspect them, then leap to her feet and follow them, laughing, when they ran to catch up with the rest of the brood.

As Anna walked quickly toward the girl, the mother hen threw up her head to see if she were a hawk, then went on about her business of feeding the chicks. "Good morning," Anna called as she approached.

The girl turned and studied Anna without interest for a moment, holding her right hand over her eyes to shade them. She wore a thin print dress and was barefooted.

"Is your mother home?" Anna asked.

"Whereabouts else would she a-went to?" the girl asked solemnly.

At first Anna was offended, thinking the child was being smart with her. Then she realized it was a simple and adequate answer to her question. "Is your mother in the house?"

"No'm." The little girl shook her head. "She's in the garden dustin her mater plants." She turned and pointed toward the barn.

Anna found the garden on the ridge above the barn, with a weathered white-oak paling fence around it. Mrs. Webber was a large woman in a faded cotton dress, wearing an old-fashioned sun bonnet. She walked from one tomato plant to the next shaking a canister above them. Dust sifted down and settled on the leaves of the plants like gray ashes. Anna could see rows of onions, garden peas, and corn crossing the garden, none of the plants large, here in the mountains, for June 11. Obviously, the growing season ran much later here above 3000 feet than in Princess Anne County, now Virginia Beach, the bedroom of the Norfolk area. Mrs. Webber, glancing up, discovered Anna before she reached the garden. She set her dusting can on the ground, stripped off her work gloves, dropped them beside it, and strode toward the garden gate, smiling.

She met Anna with outstretched hand and pumped Anna's as energetically as a man might have. Despite her bonnet and its deep visor, the older woman's face looked like kid leather which had been seasoned and tanned countless summers. Neat brown wrinkles circled her eyes and extended down her cheeks like contour furrows plowed by a careful farmer. Her eyes were dark blue and sparkled with good humor.

"Well, howdy!" she said, shaking Anna's hand. "You must be Annar, Pete's widder. We all have mortally loved the DeVosses. They was fine folks, fine neighbors. I regret I didn't get to visit Maud before she had to hurry back to her ailing sis."

"It's good to meet you, Mrs. Webber," Anna said. "You—you've got a pretty garden there."

"Well, yes, but it's a mite late this year. March and May swapped places, near about. March was a pleasure, warm as could be, but May turned out to be cold and frosty. Had to keep my mater plants in the pots the longest time, this year." She looked Anna up and down. "I vow, Jay give you a good description. You are a mighty purty young woman."

Anna was suddenly embarrassed, even more than if a strange man had complimented her. "Well, thank you," she stammered, feeling a bit silly for it. "I—I don't work at it very hard."

"They's the purtiest kind, them that's naturally purty. Pete was a fine young'un." She paused and looked past Anna at the distant hills. "A fine young man. We grieved to hear about him. Looks like the Good Lord takes the wheat sometimes and leaves the tares."

"Yeah," Anna nodded, "Pete was a fine man. He talked about you-all often, with—" (She did not want to sound corny) "—with affection."

"Well, you know he practically growed up here-abouts in the summer-time. He's walked and clumb all over these hills and rid our hosses from here to yander. Him and Jay was like brothers."

"Yeah, he told me how much he loved Holy Rood Valley."

"I ain't being neighborly a-tall," the older woman affirmed. "Won't you come into the house and set a spell? I got some good ice tea in the friger-ator."

"Thank you, Mrs. Webber, but I'll take a rain

check on it. I was out walking and just thought I'd drop by and chat a moment. You finish your work while you're at it, and I'll visit another time."

"Well, all right. But you jest wait till my maters are ripe. You still here, I'll let you have a passel."

"Thanks, I'll like that."

"Annar, do you ride hossback?"

"Yes, ma'am," Anna nodded, puzzled. "I grew up on a dairy farm. I had a pony when I was ten."

"Well, I told Jay you was lonely most like, over at that cabin by yourself, day in day out. I told him to stop messin around and take you for a hossback ride one of these purty days. He didn't say so, but he lets on that he would like to accommodate you."

"That would be nice," Anna said. "I would really enjoy that. Well, it was good to meet you."

Mrs. Webber seized her hand again and shook it. "You jest come on back any old time you get lonesome. I know what it's like to lose your man. World's all of a sudden twice as big and emptier'n a martin gourd. You come back, and I'll stop and set with you, even if the house is on fire." (She pronounced it *far*).

"Thank you, Mrs. Webber—"

"Lordy, jest call me Marthie. We don't stand on no ceremony up here in these mountains."

"Well, bye, Mrs.—Martha."

"You come back, now. If Hilder sets out to foller you, don't mind. Jest shoo her on back. She's a accident of my late years. She's a mite liking, sometimes, but she minds good. Jest tell'er I'm a-calling her, and she'll come a-runnin'."

Anna's brow furrowed. Then she decided that Mrs. Webber had meant lacking when she said *liking* and that she was talking about the girl Anna had seen playing with the chicks. "All right," Anna agreed. "I'll tell her. Bye, now."

When she passed the house, the girl Mrs. Webber had called *Hilder* —meaning *Hilda,* probably—stood on the steps watching her pass, her face reflecting wonderment. Anna did not speak to her for fear the girl would follow her, and she would have to go through the ceremony of lying to her. Anna resented having to tell even a little lie for a good reason.

When she heard the loud knock on the door Wednesday morning, while she was drinking her second cup of coffee, she knew Jay Webber would be standing there with a freckled fist raised to knock again, as she opened the door. She put down the cup, crossed the floor, and opened the door. The pattern had ended. Jay lounged on the edge of the deck stroking the muzzle of the darker of the two horses that stood in the yard.

He looked from her jeans to her face and grinned. "What happened to your granny's bathrobe?"

"I slept with my clothes on last night. What're you doing up so bright and early?"

"It's 9:30."

"I repeat, so bright and early?"

"Thought I'd go for a little ride," he said. "A morning horseback ride whets the appetite."

"You ride one and take the other along as a spare?" She leaned against the door facing, her ankles crossed.

He did not respond to her kidding but looked into the woods beyond the cabin, then at the wall above her head. "I thought maybe you—It occurred to me—Well, hell," he frowned. "Mamma suggested—"

"That I was lonely and might like to go riding?"

"Yes," he nodded too many times. "That's the gospel truth. She told me to, and no excuses. I just didn't feel like telling you Mamma sent me."

"That's great! Don't sweat it. If you have the hay to mow, just show me which horse is mine. We'll get along."

"Oh, no! I mean no. You might—What I mean is, I'm free this morning. I'd be glad to go along, show you some places, if you don't mind."

"That would be fine, Jay. Wait on me for a few minutes, will you?"

Later, she came out of the house and closed the door as he led the horses to the steps. The darker mount had a blaze face and was a gelding. The red one was a mare.

"Can I help you—"

"No, thanks. I can mount," she said quickly.

Jay swung into the saddle and watched Anna mount. "Mine is named Donner," he explained. "Yours is Blitzen."

Anna laughed. "I'm afraid to ask."

He chuckled. "No, we sold Rudolph." He was quiet a moment. "Seriously, Hilda named them, and we didn't have the heart to change them."

They turned up the driveway toward the Ridge Road. "They look a little bit like Tennessee walkers," she ventured.

"They have Tennessee blood," he agreed. "But don't let them know. I like the way they canter."

Chapter VI

They crossed the side of the ridge, well below the Webber house, and came to the bottom of the slope where woods began. Here, the pasture fence consisted of rusty barbed wire, with bars made of rails, allowing an exit into a grassy wagon road beyond. Jay Webber swung down from his saddle, let one end of the bars down, and led his mount through. Anna followed, and the bars were replaced.

"This used to be a cornfield years ago." Jay, back on his mount, gestured to indicate the surrounding woods. "When we stopped tending it, trees began to take back the land. Do you notice anything unusual about them—the trees?"

Anna looked about her, a puzzled frown on her face. "Yes, most of them are the same kind. I mean, I see a few maples and sassafras, but most of them are those trees with little oval leaves growing on stems. I believe they're called *pinnate* leaves, in botany."

"Give the lady a gold-plated maple leaf," Jay called. "Those are black locusts. Hundreds of fields and pastures have returned to forest in the mountain counties. Most of the time you can tell them in this county from the other trees. Black locust trees are hardy and so damned prolific they don't give other trees much of a chance. Sometimes I get aggravated at 'em and saw down a section of them with a chain saw and start oaks and poplars and maples and such like in the clearing."

"You sound like a horticulturist," Anna said.

"I am. Also a geologist, a bugologist, what have you. You can't grow up on a farm with your eyes open and not know a lot about a lot of things. It's a special education."

"Yes, I know." They were riding flank to flank down the wagon road. Now and then one or the other leaned to the side to avoid a limb thrust farther out into the road than the others. "I grew up on a farm. I suppose I've forgotten a great deal of what I learned."

"You would." He turned his head and looked at her. "You've got to keep one foot on the land." He was silent a moment, then added, "And be half in love with it."

"I remember black locust was what Sandy Mac-Tavish's coffin is made of," Anna said suddenly.

Jay Webber laughed. "Did old man Sparr tell you that story? Yeah, farmers make posts out of black locust because a post will stay in the ground for years without rotting."

They rode in silence for several minutes. Anna was puzzled. Jay Webber did not talk like his mother and the other mountain farmers she had heard. He was probably a product of television English, but that did not account for the way he thought. She shrugged and let the subject drop, as she reined into a bridle path leading away from the wagon road to the right. They passed from the thickety jungle of black locust trees into an older forest, large oaks, hickories, and poplars towering above the sourwood and dogwood saplings, like adults above children. Sunlight hardly penetrated here at all. There was an almost chilly dampness, as though the forest season did not include a June summer. The horses' hooves were muffled by a carpet of dead leaves. Anna rode behind Jay now, neither of them speaking. She watched his shoulders and erect head as they moved only slightly, in rhythm with his mount's movements, like an appendage of the animal's back.

After a quarter of a mile, the trunks of the trees seemed to dwindle in size, and their crests huddled groundward. The skeleton-white and gray trunks of birches began to assert themselves, with here and there a larger sycamore, none of which were thick or limby with age. The terrain had leveled out, too. Instinctively, Anna had known the river would be close ahead, before she heard the gushing water. Near the river bank, the trail forked, one branch turning left, downstream, the other, upstream. Without comment, Jay Webber turned in that direction, Anna close behind.

They came out of the woods and into sunlight abruptly. The bridle path bisected a three-acre field, part of which was a garden green with onions, tomato plants, corn, and other vegetables. But Anna hardly noticed the growing things. She stared ahead at the huge two-story mansion standing on a weed-choked lawn.

The building had been painted white once, but was now gray. The roof had originally been red tile, but the color had darkened, patches of gray-green lichen and moss scabbing it here and there, a blight of old age. The architecture was box-like and simple here in the rear, enclosed between double chimneys like bookends. Although the house gave the impression of long duration, the windows were unbroken and the shutters hung straight on their hinges. Out to the right, near the forest edge, stood an ancient log barn. Near it, the smaller outbuildings had collapsed into a black mass of rotting timber, vines and weeds growing out of them. Jay Webber rode straight across the field. All Anna could see from her saddle was the horse's rump and Jay's back. Jay projected upward like the fore part of the same animal, the sun making a halo about his golden hair.

Near the house, Jay reined toward the barn, Anna following, but he stopped beneath an ancient pear tree, one fork of which was dead, and dismounted. He tied the reins of his mount loosely about a limb. Anna swung from the saddle and collapsed into his arms. Jay reacted swiftly as he caught her. She was on her feet instantly and looked at him defensively.

"Damn, I haven't ridden in years," she muttered. "I'm completely out of shape."

He took the reins of the mare and tied them about another limb. "That'll happen," he said. "You'll probably be sore tomorrow."

Suddenly, the world was filled with music. Anna stepped backward and looked upward. A mockingbird sat on the topmost twig in the green half of the pear tree, his head back, using every bird sound in his repertoire. A cardinal flickered from one branch to another, lower down. Anna lowered her head. It was as though some impulse had turned up the volume of the receiver in her head. The fields and trees around the old house were filled with birds singing. From the apple tree near the farthest edge of the lawn, from the ragged grape arbor toward the river, from the shaggy box-wood clumps arose a variety of bird voices, and below it all, in a miniature bass background, a myriad of honeybees droned about the red clover, brilliant blue chicory blossoms, and dandelions growing wild in last year's dead broomsedge, covering what had once been a landscaped lawn. And the air was filled with a sweet perfume. She knew the honeysuckle vines embracing one of the decaying outbuildings would be there before she turned to look at them.

The mansion faced upriver, up the wagon road cut through the fallow field between the river and the base of the ridge. Six massive wooden columns reared upward from the narrow front porch to support an extension of the roof, high above. Heavy double doors were set in the middle of the house, windows on either side and above. Even from where she stood, Anna could see the brick steps from the porch to a walk, which disappeared into the jungle of dead and green broomsedge and weeds, halfway across the lawn.

Jay Webber had not spoken for several minutes. Anna guessed he was waiting to see what effect the place had on her. She turned, sucking in a gasp of air when a quail leaped from the grass and darted away, its wings drumming the air.

"Well, what do you think of Riverglade?" he asked, finally.

"I don't think anything," she said. "I might tell you part of what I feel."

"Then tell me."

"I feel nostalgia for a past I was no part of. I feel sad because it's dead. But I'm also a little annoyed. I resent the owner of this place, whoever he is, leaving it in this condition. Damnit, it's—obscene. It's like leaving a corpse to rot in the sun. Corpses ought to be cremated, or they ought to be buried with loving care."

He turned his head to look at her, his eyes narrowed thoughtfully. "What would you want him to do—the owner?"

"Either burn the place down," she said emphatically, "or fix it the hell up. I know fifty families that would grab the opportunity to live in one or two of its rooms."

Jay Webber chuckled. "You have very strong opinions, don't you, ma'am?"

"I despise waste," Anna said. "And I abhor wasted beauty." She started to put it in words that he would understand, but he interrupted.

"You think the old place is really beautiful?"

"Yes," she nodded. "Because of what it used to be and could be again."

They reached the house, and she stood on the bottom step facing him. As he stood on the walk, their eyes were almost level. "There could be a good reason for the neglect," he argued.

"I can't imagine what."

"Suppose, for example, it has been tied up in litigation, between two branches of a family, and neither was allowed to touch it."

"That would explain it," Anna agreed. "But what a stupid way to treat it! It's like King Solomon dividing the baby, in a way."

Jay opened one of the double doors and let her enter in front of him. She stopped so suddenly, staring about her, that Jay collided with her. They were in a rectangular foyer as neat as the outside was ragged. Directly across from the doors, ten feet of wall separated two enclosed stairways, which led upward, directly away from her. A tall grandfather clock, polished but silent, stood against the wall between the stairways. The oak floor had been waxed recently. Arched doorways led from the foyer into the left and right areas of the house.

Taking her by the elbow, Jay escorted Anna across the floor, stopping in front of the grandfather clock. "What do you notice about it?" he asked.

"It's run by weights," she said. "But it's not running. The weight reached the bottom on the left chain and was never transferred to the right-hand one." She smiled. "I know how the old fellow feels sometime."

"Right. Look at his face."

"It not only tells time, but the date."

"Notice the date?"

"It stopped on January 10, 1919, at 4:34 a.m. or p.m. That must have been the precise second the weight touched bottom."

"You're a bright little detective." He rested his hand briefly on her shoulder.

She turned toward him. "I'm more curious about the inside of the building," she said. "I mean, the condition compared to the lawn. It looks as though someone is still living here, taking care of the interior."

"There is." He grinned. "Ghosts!"

"Aw, come on!" Anna laughed, then shuddered. "Ghosts don't wax floors and polish grand-father clocks."

With a slight touch of his fingers, he steered her toward the arched entrance to the left of the front door. They entered a large dining room, furnished with an elongated oval dining table in the center of the room, mahogany, she was sure. There was a china cabinet, ladderback chairs, and a huge fireplace, with an iron crane for fireplace cooking. A stack of firewood lay against the wall to one side. The kitchen and pantry were back of the dining room, a large wood-burning range dominating the kitchen. Back in the dining room, Anna noticed two kerosene lamps, one on the hewn log mantel and one in the middle of the dining table. Above the mantel was a weird painting. Anna stared at it. In brilliant colors, birds with small human heads sat in the green half of a tree, a huge black vulture looking down at them from its perch high in the dead half, gnarled human hands clutching its perch. A brilliant sun with teeth like a buzzsaw shot across the dark blue sky, a comet tail behind it. She turned to ask Jay about it, but he had returned to the foyer.

When she joined him there, he said, "I'll bet you can't figure out why they built two stairways leading upstairs so close together."

"I can't imagine." She shook her head, then turned to him with a smile. "Unless upstairs is a duplex."

He grimaced. "Damn, you're uncanny. The two halves of the house upstairs are completely separated. You have to come down here from one half to enter the other half. What I mean is, why would a sane human being divide his house like that?"

"You've got me." She shrugged. "Unless the right half didn't know what the left half was doing."

"My grandfather Lance Webber had five daughters and four sons. He was a hell-and-damnation, self-ordained part-time preacher. Even while his sons and daughters were still children, around 1905, he had the old family house remodeled. The left wing of the upstairs became the boy's quarters and right wing, the girl's quarters. The old bastard didn't trust them sleeping on the same hall. He even tore the story of Lot and his daughters out of the family Bible."

"Even my parents were never that evilminded," Anna said, "and I thought they were bad enough."

"Well, Grandpappy had got him a spawn of three with neighbors' daughters when he wasn't any more than sixteen. So he knew the temptations of the flesh."

"Those poor children!" Anna sighed. "I can't imagine what their lives must have been like."

"Come on, let me show you something."

She followed him up the right-hand stairway. At the top, it doubled back into a landing, from which a hallway extended, dividing the house from there to an end window. Four closed doors faced each other, two on either side of the hallway. Jay stopped at the first door and tapped it lightly with his knuckles. "This was the master bedroom. The parents slept in this wing with the daughters, Guardians of Virtue."

He moved to the next one, on the same side, and opened the door. Anna followed him into a neat bedroom with chintzy curtains, floral wallpaper, and a colorful hooked rug. In the far corner stood a double bed, its gingham canopy trimmed with lacy frills.

"I'd say this is—was definitely a room for girls," Anna stated. "A bit gaudy but feminine."

"This was the bedroom of Alace and Susan," Jay explained, "the two oldest daughters."

"If I ever have children—" she started to say. Turning her head, she could glimpse Jay Webber's face in the gloom. There was an expression on his face she would have recognized, even if she had never seen it on a man's face before. "*Remember, you promised to wait until I return,*" the ghost in her brain whispered. She swallowed. Clinching her fists, she turned away from him and hurried through the doorway and down the hall. Jay followed her, saying nothing.

When they reached the bottom of the stairs, he stopped. "About the clock," he said.

She turned, touched his arm, then let her hand fall. "Yes, what about the clock?"

"Grandpa Lance's family was stricken by influenza in January, 1919. There was an epidemic throughout these mountains, few people well enough to help anyone else. The whole Webber family died except for my father, who was sixteen, and one of Lance's daughters, one of those he sired with a neighbor's daughter. I forgot to tell you, when Grandpa admitted his parentage, my great-grandfather made him rear all three of them."

"You mean the woods colts?"

"If you like folk terms. Anyway, she and my dad were raised by my grandmother's family, the MacTavishes. The old house remained empty for years, at first haunted, according to local superstition. Later, tied up in litigation between Sarah, the love child, and Dad. Dad finally won."

"You mean your family owns Riverglade now?"

"I own it!" he stated. "It was all I wanted. Dad willed it and eighty acres across the river to me. I've been working on the house, inside, when I could find time, but I haven't had a chance to clean up outside yet, except for the garden."

"Look, Jay, I'm sorry about what I said. I mean about whoever owned the place. I didn't know—"

"Oh, that's okay." He laughed and turned toward the front door. "You were right, of course, without the facts." Suddenly he whirled on her, concern on his face. "For God's sake, don't tell my mother—don't tell *anyone* what I said about grandpa and his daughters. My mother doesn't want it talked about. You know how proud mountain people are. I don't know what made me do it. I know better."

"The devil made you do it," Anna said, but he did not seem amused.

When they were halfway across the lawn, he stopped and pointed. "See those two flowers there?"

She looked at the tall stalks, each topped by a circular pattern of white flowers made up of countless smaller blooms.

"Do they look alike to you?"

"Yes. They look like Queen Anne's lace to me."

"Look again."

She studied them. "No, the one on the right has a smoother pattern. It looks like a neat lace doily. The other one is ragged in outline. There's a small black flower—"

"Purple," Jay said.

"There's a small purple blossom precisely in the center of the nearer one."

"Very good, Mrs. DeVoss," he said solemnly. "That's Queen Anne's lace. The other flower is common yarrow. It has a shallow root structure." He stepped forward, stooped, and pulled up the Queen Anne's lace, holding it toward her. The green stem ended in a small, elongated tuber. "Queen Anne's lace is also called wild carrot."

"Well, thank you, Professor, for today's lesson in botany."

"If you ever have to run for it," he said, "you can eat them—the wild carrots."

"Thanks, but I'll take along fried chicken."

A short distance beyond the lawn, as they rode upriver, Jay reined into a well-worn path that led toward the base of the ridge. Anna followed. The little cemetery, enclosed by a zigzag rail fence black with age, was clean and well kept, although the graves, all except one, were obviously old. Some of the marble tombstones were discolored near their bases by moss. The new grave, perhaps a year or two old, had a double monument with the vital statistics of J.W. Webber on it. The other half contained the name Martha MacTavish Webber b. 1910 d.—

"There are many family cemeteries in Watauga County," Jay explained. "West of Boone, along Highway 421, you'll see them crowning beautiful little knolls, with fences around them."

"I wonder why," Anna mused aloud.

"Perhaps because folks used to die in the home, and it was simpler to bury them nearby." Jay spoke thoughtfully. "Then again, families used to be closer than nowadays. They couldn't let their loved ones go entirely, even after they had died."

"I like that explanation better," she said.

Chapter VII

Anna DeVoss was reminded of Jay Webber for the next three days because of her sore behind, but she did not see him for the rest of that week. He crossed her mind now and then, usually in relation to the old mansion, Riverglade. There were some things she was still curious about, some questions unanswered, but they did not stimulate her curiosity enough to goad her to any action. When the escapade of Lance Webber, his grandfather, and the neighbors' girls slipped into her mind from some vague association, she would deliberately shuttle it aside, except for the irony of it, which amused her. But she felt more secure not thinking about it at all.

Around noon on Friday, a thunderstorm hove into view from Tennessee, the southern perimeter passing over Holy Rood Valley. There was a great deal of thunder and lightning, but not much rain. When it had passed, sputtering and grumbling like a man splashed by a passing car, Anna drove to Sparr's Store for some sugar, milk, and a small bag of meal. She sat with Henry Sparr and a tobacco farmer named Simon Tull for over an hour listening to them talk about the old days in Watauga County, asking an occasional question. She was fascinated by the story of the narrow-gauge railroad and the little train called Tweetsie, which had once run from east Tennessee to Boone. The 1940 flood had washed away miles of track and much of the roadbed, terminating the train's career. It ended up as a tourist ride on Highway 321 near Blowing Rock. Anna tried to imagine a time when the roads were narrow and muddy and only Model-T Fords were around to use them—a time when a young man from the tobacco factory in Winston-Salem had driven his Ford two miles up the bed of Cove Creek to visit his girl friend because there was no road to her father's house, a time when the main street in Boone was so deep in mud a chicken trying to cross it got mired and had to be rescued.

There was an earlier time, Simon Tull told her, when a stagecoach ran from Blowing Rock to Linville, in Avery County, along the old Yonahlossee Trail, now Highway 221, hauling wealthy summer people to their summer places or to the lodges then in existence.

As she was leaving the store, a black and chrome Mercedes-Benz, shining like a polished hearse, stopped beside the car. She had looked away from it as she descended the steps, when a man called to her.

"Hey, there, Mrs. DeVoss—Anna!"

Reaching the ground, she looked up. Mark

Grunwald, dressed in white shirt, tie, blue linen coat, and white trousers, stood beside the black car, his hand on top of the open door. Christ on Monday! she thought. I knew he would be driving a twenty thousand dollar Mercedes.

"Hi," she said, as she approached her car. "What brings you out into the boondocks?"

He closed the door and hurried around the front of his car, meeting her close to her own vehicle. "I want to apologize," he said. "Betty—you know, the receptionist at Grayhound—she told me you really did not have a telephone. I thought you were just—just cutting me off."

And that's how you salved your wounded male ego, she thought. Women just don't cut Mark Grunwald off like that. "No need to apologize," she said. "It's not important."

"It's important to me. I was just stopping here to get directions to your chalet."

"You mean you drove all the way out here just to apologize for not believing me?"

His dark eyes flickered away toward the roof of the old store, then back to her face. "Well, yes, that and—I had another, better reason."

"Which is?"

"I wanted to invite you to dinner at the lodge Saturday evening, and to the dance afterwards. I realize it's not exactly traditional to wait until Friday to ask for a Saturday evening date, but I talked to Betty just this morning."

"Who worries about traditions this late in the century?" Anna remarked. She was thoughtful a moment. "I had planned to—" Actually, she had no plan at all. She was not particularly ecstatic about going out with this formal tycoon. On the other hand, a male companion for a change, a *safe* male companion and an evening out were better than doing nothing. The silent cabin was beginning to depress her just a little.

Apparently to influence what he took to be indecision on her part, Mark Grunwald said, "If I said *please*, if I promised you a good time—"

Anna laughed. "Not really, if I had other plans I couldn't break. But I haven't. Okay, I'll go."

"How about eight o'clock?" He grasped her left arm eagerly, then released it and thrust his offending hand into his coat pocket. "I mean, could I pick you up around eight?"

"That would be fine. I'll expect you at eight tomorrow evening, right?"

After she had explained to him how to find the DeVoss cabin, she drove back with diverse emotions troubling her. The fact that she wanted to be alone, did not want to go out with Mark Grunwald, so evenly balanced a need to escape the lonely cabin for an evening that she could not have explained why she agreed to go. In fact, at the moment, she wished she had not agreed, but it was too late to change her mind. She did not see any easy way out of the date. Oh, why not? she thought. It'll be more interesting than listening to stories about Jay Webber and his weird ancestors, even if he decided to come by, and he probably would not.

All day Saturday the sky was obliterated by the gray wool of fog, now and then great skeins of it breaking loose, to fall away and be blown northeast as it coiled and writhed like steam from a boiling cauldron. From time to time sunlight would break· through as a bright surprise, before the hole in the sky was quickly plugged. Anna tried to hurry time by reading at Butterfly Falls, but it was cool in the forest, and the weather depressed her. Now, she found herself actually looking forward to the evening out, even if Mark Grunwald did not exactly stimulate her to excitement.

He drove into one of the parking bays at precisely eight o'clock, as she had known he would. She had been ready for half an hour, but to prevent the wrong impression, she left him in a chair by the fireplace while she sat on the closed commode lid fiddling with her nails. Finally, she was ready. Mark Grunwald leaped to his feet when she re-entered the living room. He was being very conservative with her this evening, wearing a dark suit rather than a bright jacket, as she had seen him dressed before.

"My, but you look pretty tonight, Anna," he said. "You'll turn heads at the lodge."

"Thank you." She smiled, glancing down at herself. She had to admit she really did look good, dressed for the first date after—after burying the past. The flimsy little cocktail dress with its short skirt revealed as much of her body and legs as good taste allowed—did not so much *reveal* as *presented*. The white cleavage swelled into the V-neckline, and her long, round calves were contoured by the silver-flecked stockings. Pete would have loved the way she was dressed tonight. She smiled whimsically. He would have slipped up behind her, embraced her, and waltzed her around the room on her tiptoes, while she tried to slap at him with both hands. They always arrived at a party late. She looked up into the face of her escort, and the memory of Pete DeVoss slowly faded.

Their conversation was desultory on the way to the lodge. Mark Grunwald played his cards with tact, taking his stance somewhere between not quite formal and almost familiar. The lobster, flown in to the golf course runway from Maine, was delicious, better than any she had ever eaten in Norfolk. The dining room was almost full. She supposed it was because of the dance after dinner.

A woman in her early thirties stopped by their table once, towing her heavy husband like a motorboat pulling a barge.

"Oh, Mark, it's so good to run into you again. You're as handsome as ever. When did you come up? Are you—"

Mark Grunwald stood, waiting for her to run down before he spoke. "It's good to see you,

Beatrice. Hello, George." He shook hands quickly with the husband. "Beatrice and George Wayne, I'd like you to meet Anna DeVoss."

"How do you do." Anna's smile flickered on and off.

"Oh, Anna, I bet you're Pete's wid—widow. I did so want to meet you. We have the A-frame below the DeVoss cabin. I wanted you over sometime for bridge."

"I'm sorry, I play only poker," Anna said. "Pete was a military man."

But Beatrice Wayne was not a woman to wait for explanations. "We were so sorry to hear about poor Pete, weren't we, Honey?" She nudged George with her elbow, and he nodded in agreement. "That was such a nasty war. Only the best and bravest, you know. I haven't seen—hadn't seen Pete since we were both quite young, but we were very close. Mom and Dad loved him dearly."

Anna's smile had come back and stretched across her teeth like rubber bands. She tried to imagine Pete involved with this woman, even ten or fifteen years earlier, but could not visualize it. Beatrice was just not Pete DeVoss's type.

"It was good of you to drop by our table," Mark Grunwald said. "We'll have to get together later and bring things up to date."

Beatrice Wayne blinked up at him a moment, then said, "Indeed, we will. Great to have met you, Anna. You'll hear from me later." She hurried away, escorting George by the arms as though he were under arrest.

Mark sat back down, shaking his head. "God, I'm sorry. Looks like I got you into something."

"It wasn't your fault. Besides, I can take care of the world's Beatrice Waynes."

"I bet you can," he laughed, and for a moment Anna saw a relaxed side of him she liked.

The dance floor was too small and too crowded, the combo was too fast for the clientele, and Mark Grunwald danced as though he wore golf shoes. Anna counteracted her disappointment by drinking too much Jack Daniels and branch water. She was quite tipsy by eleven thirty. She was introduced to several couples who lived in chalets about the mountain side, but she remembered none of the names. She was so miserable trying to follow the big, awkward buckdancer she was actually relieved when he suggested that they go to his place for conversation and a nightcap. By now, she was in a tranquil stupor and ready to do almost anything but try to dance.

The Grunwald chalet was only a few hundred yards up the side of the mountain, anchored to the top of a massive rock. While Anna stood on the deck, her hands braced on the railing, and looked down across the dark roofs below her toward the club house and the golf course beyond, her host was busy lighting a fire to wood already laid in the fireplace. He joined her a little later carrying two tall, cool glasses, handing one to her. "This is the Grunwald special," he laughed, "Guaranteed to make you happier."

"But I'm always happy," Anna protested. "Can't you tell?"

"This'll make you happier than you always are."

"Okay, we'll just see about that." She sipped the drink, rolling it about with her tongue. It had a minty flavor and was light and bubbly, like champagne. "Hey! it really is good." She took another longer gulp, savored it a moment, then swallowed it. And then another.

They returned to the den and sat on the fluffy rug before the flickering little fire. Mark Grunwald had turned the lights out, and the stereo speakers emitted soft music from somewhere in the darkness on either side of them. It was a very peaceful setting, and Anna felt suddenly secure, although a latent understanding told her to be alert. Alcohol had subdued, for the time being, the old sadness and had rendered her guard impotent. She even forgot what a miserable dancer Mark Grunwald had been because it was so far in the past it no longer mattered.

"Feel good, Anna?" he asked softly.

"Very good, thank you. Most excellent."

"What do you do when you are working? I can usually guess, but you puzzle me."

Anna turned her head to look at him, but he was serious. The firelight splashing against his dark profile gave him a handsome, exotic appearance, as though he were some Bohemian prince, she thought dreamily, who had escaped to America to become a commoner.

"I was a social worker. Am, because I have a leave of absence. I majored in English, though. Specifically, I work with abused children."

"That fits." He snapped his fingers. "There's a kind of compassion deep in your eyes. Why didn't I think of that before?"

"Because," Anna laughed, "you are a Bohemian prince who escaped to America."

"What?" He stared at her. "Oh, now I get it."

"Just a peasant joke." She threw back her head and laughed a strangled little laugh, the skin tight across her throat. "I've got a weird sense of humor, Mark, and I don't share it with anyone else. You'll just have to forgive me." She was silent a moment, "And what do you do, Sir Prince, when you're working—IF you work."

"I'm manager of a line of knitting mills." He paused, apparently for her reaction, then continued when she did not speak. "And first vice-president."

"Well, good." Anna yawned. "I've gone and caught me an executive type."

She looked up into his face. He was studying her, his brow furrowed. "Don't you like executive types?"

"I like men," she said. "But I like men of action,

most. Were you always a tall, dark, and handsome bachelor?" She took three rapid swallows of her drink, emptying the glass.

"Do you mean, am I or was I ever married?" He sounded peeved. "The answer is yes. I'm divorced. My ex-wife lives in Alabama with our daughter."

"I don't have a daughter," Anna said softly. "All I have is a photograph. My children are still crosswise in my heart and can't ever, ever escape."

"What do you like to do most?" he asked quietly.

"I love to sit before a fire drinking with a tall, dark, and handsome Bohemian prince," she murmured, "and forget about my children who never got born."

He took the empty glass from her hand and set it aside, then placed his own with it. When he put his arms about her and forced her slowly, slowly backward onto the rug, she did not resist. When he kissed her, she responded, though with little passion.

"Wait for me until I return," the ghost voice whispered.

Her mind came flashing back from outer space, cold and alert. She whirled away from him and was on her hands and knees facing him before he could make a movement to retreat. He was sitting up and staring at her in bewilderment. "What did I do wrong?" he stammered.

For a moment she was angry, but mostly with herself. Then it left her as she looked into his dark face splotched by firelight and understood him. "Nothing, Mark," she said quietly. "You did everything right—the drinks, the music, the fire. It's me. I'm just not ready yet. I don't know why. It's probably stupid, but I'm not ready."

"I wouldn't have offended you for—"

She put her hand over his mouth. They stood together. She hugged him and kissed him on the cheek. "It's not you. Don't feel disappointed in yourself. It's me. I'm just—I don't know what's wrong with me. Would you be a good guy and take me home?"

"Sure, Anna, anything you say." Her explanation seemed to satisfy him. "I—I think I understand."

"If you do, I wish to God you'd explain it to me."

They rode back to Holy Rood Valley mostly in silence. The alcohol had fled Anna's brain, leaving it as clear as a winter night. When she turned at the cabin door, he was staring down at her like a lost little boy.

"Can I see you again?" he asked.

"We'll see," she smiled. "When you think it over, you may not want to see me again."

Reaching up, she pulled his head down and kissed him lightly, then turned and entered the cabin, closing the door behind her. Moving over to the window beside the fireplace, she stood in the darkness and watched his taillights disappear through the trees. "Thus endeth the chapter entitled 'Mark Grunwald, Bohemian Prince, who Escaped to America and Became Vice-President of a Chain of Knitting Mills'," she muttered.

In her bedroom, she picked up the photograph of Pete and studied it a long time. She felt good because she was almost sure he smiled his approval of her escape and winked. But when she thought it over, in bed alone, she realized that Lieutenant Pete DeVoss did not or would not have thought like that.

Chapter VIII

When Anna woke up on Monday morning with a pain in her back and her abdomen seething, she knew what had happened. Her mother had called it "the Condition." Was it just yesterday? Could it have been over six years ago, really? Anna would say, "I'm sorry, Sweet," and she would kiss Pete. "But no trespassing. I'm sorry."

And he would say, "Damn that Eric the Red. How I'd love to get him in my bombsight!"

By the time she drank her third cup of coffee, her head had begun to ache. She took two aspirins to relieve it, but the nagging pain in her back persisted. She had just cleaned her teeth and washed her hands when Jay Webber knocked on the cabin door. She knew it was Jay from the rhythm and from the number of knocks, which she did not count but tabulated subconsciously. He was standing there in the same faded jeans and shirt (or did he have a wardrobe of them?) holding in his hands, cradled against his side, a large paper bag half full of something she could not see because of the bag's crumpled top.

"Well, good morning, Jay," she smiled. "Are you delivering groceries these days?" She was not particularly exuberant to see him or anyone else, with her nagging back pain.

For the briefest of moments his eyes narrowed. Then he smiled. "No, I have a surprise for you—if you're willing to be surprised."

"I like *nice* surprises. Come on in."

He entered and she closed the door while he carried the bag over to the sink. "You know what this brown thing is I'm totin?" he called over his shoulder.

"It's a paper bag of surprises." She followed him and stopped near the lazy-Susan.

"No. Hit hain't." He set the bag down on the counter beside the sink and turned, grinning. "Hit's a paper *poke*, in Holy Rood Valley."

"I thought that word went out with Hoover."

"Well, smartie, I have to admit it's not used as much as it used to be." He looked a bit crestfallen.

She shrugged. "What's the surprise?"

"Not till later. Do you have anything planned this morning?"

"Not the teeniest. Are we going back to the ancestral manor and hear sad stories of the deaths of Webbers?"

He searched her face, his amber eyes wide and vulnerable. When she smiled to prove she was only kidding, his grin filled the space between beard and mustache, spilling into the funnels of his eyes. "No, I want to show you something else. But we'll have to go out to Butterfly Falls. Do you mind?"

"Not at all. I like it there. It's a last wilderness-like."

"Abe MacTavish came into Holy Rood Valley before the Civil War," Jay said, as they followed the path out to the creek. "He bought thousands of acres of land at a dollar or so an acre. He hewed logs with a broadax and built a house. Then he went over into Kentucky to the cabin of Big Bear Bowman, who had ten daughters, and told him and his wife he wanted to pick him a *steady* wife. He meant *sturdy*. Said he would pay five hundred dollars for the right one. Big Bear took the money and told Abe to take his pick. In spite of the wife's fussing, Abe MacTavish made the girls strip down to the buff, and he proceeded to select his wife. He squeezed their thighs, measured them from hip to hip, checked their pelvic area—and chose Essie, next to the youngest, who was sixteen. They were married by a circuit preacher under a blooming service berry tree, and Abe brought Essie back to his house. It stood just about where Riverglade stands. Essie had her first child in nine months and two days after marriage and Abe delivered it himself."

"She had thirteen more, nine girls and five boys. Abe MacTavish rode a mule when he was eighty-two, crisscrossing his land and divided it up into sections, blazing trees with a hatchet to mark boundaries. He gave one section to each of his children. The girls married into other families, taking their portion of land with them. Two of the boys were killed in the Civil War, one with the South and one, in Tennessee, with the North. Great Uncle Sandy MacTavish never married. Great-grandmother Selina MacTavish married Great-grandfather Roan Webber. That's where our land came from."

Anna stopped abruptly, seizing Jay's arm and dragging him to a halt. "Are you kidding me?" she demanded.

He stared at her, on guard. "What do you mean?"

"I mean about Abe MacTavish feeling and groping those poor girls like he was buying a mule, to choose a wife. Because if you are kidding, just because I'm from outside, I resent it."

"Aw, come on, Anna!" He took her arm and escorted her several steps along the trail. "Why would I do that?" A few strides later, he laughed suddenly. "I figure trying to fool you would be a waste of time. Do I really look stupid enough to try?"

"I have no idea what you would try to do," she said. "I hardly know you at all."

"Don't blame me for that." He paused. "You're the one who likes to be alone."

"Did he, sure enough, though?" she asked, looking up into his face as they walked. "Did Abe really choose his wife like that? Why didn't he just look at their teeth?"

"Great-grandmother Selina told Grandpa it was like that. Nobody would dispute her word. Besides, it wasn't teeth old Abe was interested in. It was an incubator."

"You mean a young woman's child-bearing ability?"

"Yes, that's true."

"The old chauvinist bastard must have been thirty years older than that poor little girl. That's what happens living in an age when men are supreme and women are only chattel."

"She wasn't any weakling," Jay Webber argued. "Fourteen children in twenty-two years."

"Sixteen and twenty-two's only thirty-eight. Why did she stop having children? I bet it wasn't old Abe's idea."

"I'm afraid to tell you." He grinned.

She halted beside the creek, dragging him to a stop. "Why? I've got to know."

"You would swear I was pulling your leg, sure enough."

"Come on, now. Why? We'll stand here all day."

"Old Abe came down with the mumps while he was on a hunting trip."

"You mean—"

"They fell on him, as the folks say. He became sterile."

"You're right about one thing."

"What?"

"You really are pulling my leg."

"I swear by Holy Rood Rock."

Anna DeVoss threw back her head, her laughter rushing toward the treetops. "Boy, if that isn't poetic justice! If it hadn't been for the mumps, everyone in this county would have been named MacTavish." She stopped laughing and faced him. "You're not kidding me, Jay Webber? Not really?"

Jay held up his hands, palms up. "So help me, John the Baptist!"

"Man, you really have a heritage, don't you? Between Great-grandpa Abe MacTavish and Grandpa Lance Webber, I don't see how they can afford to let you run loose."

"I'm very normal, Anna," he said quickly. "I live one day at a time, and I have no enemies."

She stared at him quizzically, started to say something else, but could think of no response.

When they reached the pool beneath the trees, Jay walked over to the edge of the woods and picked up what looked to Anna like two switches. But when he returned and held them out to her, she could see they were small limbs from a thorn bush. They had been trimmed down smooth, except at the base of each, two thorns were left, forming hooks when he held them by their small ends. The bark on the limbs was still green and moist where torn. They had obviously been cut recently and left near the pool that morning.

"I know what they are, but what are they for?" she asked.

"What do you think they are?"

"Thorn limbs," she said, "with thorns left on them."

"No ma'am. You lose. They are Cherokee fish-hooks."

"Fishhooks? No smart fish would bite one of those things."

"They don't work like that. You just sit here on the rock, be as quiet as a baby quail, and watch Big Chief Webber catch heap big fish, maybe two, for our dinner."

"Why don't you just use a hook and fly?"

"No sport in that. Besides, after the Big *Boom,* there won't be any more hooks and flies. Just thorns."

She started to needle him further about the thorns, but he had moved away. She sat down on the sloping rock and watched him tiptoe toward the embankment adjacent to the waterfall. Only a foot above the pool, a shelf of rock began and slanted upward away from its surface. Jay Webber lay down on the rock, placing one of the thorn limbs aside and keeping the other. He lay with his chest against the rock, only his head and hand projecting out over the water. With his right hand, he held onto the the small end of the limb and extended it with the thorns on it below the surface of the pool. Then he lay quietly, an extension of the stone on which he reclined. Anna squinted through her sunglasses trying to see into the water where the thorns waited, but she could discern nothing.

Jay Webber waited and Anna waited. She did not know how long. Little numb disks began to form where her backsides flattened against the rock. She squirmed, walking forward a few inches with her buttocks. She gasped suddenly, one hand flying upward to trap the sound inside of her mouth. Jay had moved so fast the action was over before she could focus on him. His right arm rose in the air, and the twin thorns had hooked a trout *under* its mouth. In one smooth motion, the fish sailed over Jay's shoulder, hurled by the thorn limb, and fell halfway up the rock, where it now lay flopping and beating with a wet fish sound. Jay got up, walked to it, and with the side of his foot, flung the speckled trout farther away from the pool, where it could exhaust its panic with little chance of escaping back into the water.

Anna got up and walked over to Jay. "How in the world did you do that? I've never heard of that kind of fishing before."

When she met his eyes, Anna glimpsed a boyish pleasure. (Look, little girl, see how far I can jump.) "It's a matter of timing and patience," he explained. "You hold the thorns beneath the surface until a trout swims nearby. Then you ease it into position, yank upward and flip at the same time, and behold! you have part of a meal."

"Well, I must say, it's a clever idea." She stood with her right hip outthrust, her hand on it. "But I don't know many people who could lie still that long."

"There aren't many anymore," Jay said. "There used to be many tribes of them."

"Who ever heard of a red-haired, kinky-headed Indian?"

Jay grinned. "I'm the last of the Peckerwood Tribe. Now get back over there in your place, squaw woman, so I can catch another."

When Jay had caught four trout, weighing over a pound each, he strung three of them on one of the thorn hooks and stored the other in the crotch of a sourwood tree. Then they returned to the cabin with the catch, after Jay had cleaned them on a stump beside the creek, throwing the scraps into the water for other fish to eat.

While Anna hovered just out of reach, feeling unnecessary and a little stupid, Jay Webber fried the trout, rolled in corn meal, and made slaw from a cabbage head he had brought in the paper bag. While the fish were frying, he had a small iron skillet on a back burner, baking cornbread.

Anna said very little during the meal because she ate ravenously. She had little patience for empty words at mealtime. Part of it was that she was hungry. Part of it was that any meal she did not have to prepare herself was usually good. But this food was special. She had grown up near the beach, where seafood was commonplace. However, there was a special savor about mountain trout caught with primitive skill, fried in corn meal, and served with fresh slaw and cornbread. Jay did not attempt to start a conversation. He was busy eating himself. But she caught him watching her eat, now and then, and there was a pleased look about his eyes. When they were through, Anna served the coffee, which had been perking while they ate. They went outside and sat on the deck, their feet on the log steps, while they drank it.

"How'd you like that?" Jay asked, finally, across his cup.

"How'd I like *what*?"

"Come on! You know."

"You mean the coffee?"

"Yeah, the coffee, ma'am. This is my third cup."

Anna laughed at him. "If you expect me to compliment you on that meal, forget it. I don't have the words to describe it."

"You really liked it, then?"

"Come on, Jay! You know how good it was. You watched me making a pig of myself."

Jay laughed, a deep, comfortable laugh, setting his cup down with a bang. "You're one hell of a flatland broad. I bet you punched your mother's breast while you were nursing."

Anna felt a small flush of resentment at his remark, but let it pass. At the moment she was too content to be bothered by anything very long. Her stomach was pleasantly gorged, and she felt a drowsy euphoria despite the coffee. "What gave you the idea I had a mother?"

He laughed a scoffing little laugh. "Even Anna DeVoss couldn't bear herself."

She looked at him closely, but his face was relaxed, without malice. There was a distant look in his eyes, as though he too were drowsy, and she felt herself doubting that he even realized what he had said.

"Jay," she said quietly, "how well did you know Pete?"

He stared at her, his face taut, on guard. She had the feeling he was trying to judge how much to say, whether or not she would burst out bawling like some broken-hearted widow. "Pretty well," he said, finally. "He was older than me. We rode horseback together, fished together, once we even—Oh, hell, I can't tell you that."

"Can't tell me what? I insist."

"Way back when we were kids, Dad and Dr. DeVoss would set up a pot in the woods and cook brunswick stew. Squirrel, rabbit, quail, chicken, beef, pork, vegetables—Lord, it was good! I can taste it now. The DeVosses were the only summer people in the valley then. Some of the neighbors would come over. We would eat until the food ran out our ears. The grown-ups would drink home-brew or white lightning and get happy as chickens on a Junebug farm. No foolishness, though. No one ever got mad. Just good old fashioned drinking and picking and singing. Old hymns and old ballads." He stopped and stared for several moments out through the trees. "Boy, Dad missed those days toward the end. He had a stroke and was bedridden for a while before he died. He used to laugh out of one side of his mouth and talk about the good old days when he and Dr. DeVoss drank together and made brunswick stew and all that. He died fretting because the modern summer people thought of him as just a grit, a peckerwood tobacco farmer not worth talking to."

"Did you like Pete?" Anna asked.

Jay Webber studied her with a peculiar slanting look. "How could I not like him? How could anyone not like him? There wasn't a malicious bone in his body. Christ, he loved life and living things. He would think up new things to do that would never cross my mind." He paused. "You know, I could never put him and a military plane together, in my mind."

"Jay, tell me something." Anna caught his eyes and held them.

"Sure thing. What?"

"What did you start to say a few minutes ago, then changed the subject? You said, 'Once we even—' then stopped. What were you going to say?"

"I'd better not tell you. It might embarrass you."

"I'm hard to embarrass, Jay. Nothing about my husband would embarrass me."

"Damn, you're a tough female to deal with."

"Come on, tell me. What do you think I am, a Girl Scout? That man was my first and only lover. He would have been the father of my children, if that asinine brawl in Vietnam hadn't—had not taken him. I want to know everything about him I can find out."

Jay lowered his head, scuffing his ragged sneakers against the step. "It wasn't much, really. When we were about fourteen, he gave Beatrice Paulson—she's Beatrice Wayne now—ten dollars to strip in front of him and me at Butterfly Falls. Gad, I feel like a pervert now."

"Come on, Jay. You were only children."

Jay laughed. "Pete got cheated. It wasn't worth any ten dollars, I'll tell you that."

Anna threw back her head and laughed, her voice gushing toward the tree tops, too high on the scale for humor alone. "That's old Pete. That's my man. He always got to the point—wasted no time." She calmed abruptly, her voice lower. "And I agree with you. I'm sure ten dollars was too much. Ninety-eight cents probably was."

Jay grinned. "You know Beatrice?"

"I met her Saturday night. She doesn't look like much of a catch, even at thirty-three, or whatever she is."

"She had enough to catch old George Wayne."

"She could have done that with a forked limb." Anna stretched and yawned. "Jay, I hate to do this, but I'm going to have to take a nap."

He looked at her covertly, but she caught his eyes. "You don't need company, I don't reckon."

She smiled at him, stood up. "You're welcome to the other bedroom."

He got to his feet, too. "You wouldn't mind? I mean, me in the next room, sleeping?"

"Why should I?" She studied him intently. "I don't mind and the trees don't mind. What could it hurt?"

"Very likely, not a damned thing," he said. "I'd just as soon go on back to the house and get to work."

"Suit yourself, Jay-boy." Reaching over, she ruffled his kinky hair with her right hand. "I do appreciate the meal, and it *was* delicious. You're a real neighbor. If the Big *Bang* ever does come, thanks to you I can catch trout with a Cherokee fishhook."

"See you later, *neighbor*." He threw her a quick salute and descended the steps. She watched him for half a minute, as he headed up the driveway through the woods, never looking back. Then she entered the cabin and closed the door.

Chapter IX

Anna had read about the annual "Singing on the Mountain" in the *Watauga Democrat,* the county newspaper, during the week and thought it might be interesting to attend it. Pete had once told her that it was a descendant of the old camp meetings and singings, a real folk artifact. She awakened around six-thirty on Sunday and dressed rapidly, hoping to beat most of the heavy traffic expected on the fiftieth anniversary of the occasion. A local man had organized the first Singing with the motto: "Whoever would may come." The invitation had been taken literally. Over the years the number attending the Singing, in McRae Meadows, near the western base of Grandfather Mountain, had gradually increased, as governors and other public figures were added to the program, until now thousands made the June pilgrimage each year.

Anna's reason for attending was to get a taste of the old fashioned religious folk singing, a way of worshipping—in her imagination—as native to the mountains as the rugged individuals who participated. Her first mistake, she decided later, was attending at all, especially the fiftieth anniversary.

Her second was not leaving the cabin an hour earlier than she did. She was caught in a traffic jam a mile long and ended up parking in the Town of Linville, near the highway which led to the Singing. Cars were lined up bumper to bumper in three directions, reaching out of sight. As it was, she had to walk about two miles to McRae Meadows, but fortunately had worn a pair of sneakers. It was worse than Saturday afternoon at a Carolina football game, she decided. But she was not alone. She was swept along in a river of pilgrims, from the ancient to babes in arms, and all ages between, from all levels of society. They moved with one purpose, laughing, joking, singing, bitching about the long hike, but none of them with the remotest intention of turning back.

The young redheaded teenager in front of her sang in a sweet soprano:

> Who will shoe your little feet,
> and who will glove your hand;
> who will kiss your rosy red cheek
> when I'm in a far-off land?
> The storms blow over the ocean,
> the heavenly peace would be;
> the world would lose its motion, dear,
> if I prove false to thee.

The leaders of the Singing occupied two platforms on two huge rocks uphill from where the audience (or congregation) stood, sat, or sprawled in lawn chairs or on blankets, coats, or pieces of newspapers. Anna sat on the corner of a patchwork quilt occupied by a young couple and their little boy. She stared curiously about her, her ears attuned to the patterns of speech, from mountain dialect to sophisticated Yankee English. There were two other giant boulders, one beside those holding the platforms and one behind them. God had prepared a convenient stage for the service, at the beginning of the world, Anna mused. A zigzag rail fence surrounded most of the tilted meadow. Over to her left was an open shed with a sign which read: AVERY COUNTY RESCUE SQUAD. Looking back to her right, she studied Grandfather, or what was seen as Grandfather Mountain from other perspectives. The old man of the mountains had disappeared. Here, close below his chin, he had become three massive peaks, chin, nose, and forehead, without pattern, jutting up into the swollen bellies of passing clouds.

Because of the size of the congregation and the traffic problem, the program did not get underway until around noon. Earlier, the sky had been clear, although the persistent breeze was cool. But by eleven, clouds were tumbling out of the west, each rank larger and darker than the last, so that the sky was cloudy by twelve. Anna kept glancing upward distrustfully. It would just be her luck to get her tail soaked while caught in a stampede of human buffalos as far as she could see, over forty thousand, she heard one old timer estimate.

She sat through the performance of a string band from Charlotte, the short speech of General Westmoreland (candidate for governor of South Carolina), and the clichés of Bob—"Singing on the Mountain"—Hope. By the time the governor of North Carolina began to preach his sermonette condemning "mere Sunday Christians," she had made up her mind to get the hell out before the rain started. She already knew more than enough about folk singing on the mountain. Johnny Cash settled it, although she could see from the rapt faces of those around her that he was what they had come to see and hear—not folk hymns nor ex-generals nor governors nor perennial comedians, but Johnny Cash.

She thanked the couple, got to her feet, and walked a crooked path among the spectators, the flat tones of "Will the Circle be Unbroken," magnified many times and rolling across the throng, to collide with Grandfather's rugged chin, now wrapped in a wreath of torn clouds. Anna was disgusted with herself and disappointed with the whole day. Somewhere over the years, the "Singing on the Mountains" had lost its native purpose, she sensed, and had gone tourist. She could see with a sweep of her eyes as she walked among them that most of the spectators (not congregation) here were either summer people or city folk who had driven into the mountains for this special occasion, all of them famished for any publicized entertainment. The backdrop of Grandfather and the green forests of the Blue Ridge, for the throng, could as easily have been painted on a piece of canvas stretched across a stage as a background for Johnny Cash, the center of "worship."

She had almost reached the outer fringes of the massed audience when Anna felt a strange flutter at the base of her throat. Off to her left, with a pretty redhead, Jay Webber sat on a blanket, his eyes on the distant platform and the high priest in a black smock. Anna had not recognized him at first, although her eyes had, because he was dressed in a white shirt and dark trousers. She would have known him without a second glance, in his usual farm clothing. Her first impulse was to go over and talk to him for a few minutes. But a second look at his companion, who clutched his arm as though she thought he would escape, changed her mind. She continued to wade through sprawling bodies and outflung legs.

It was almost two-thirty when she reached her car. She had just moved out onto the highway, heading toward Boone, when the sky unzipped to baptize the green world and her vehicle in a shower of cold rain. Jehovah, on his day, had not dealt kindly with the outdoor singing. The world Dr. DeVoss had loved, that Pete had hurried through as a child, was dying. She found herself wondering how long it would take for the old folkways of this region to become plastic imitations for the summer people.

On the following Wednesday, Anna was rummaging beneath some blankets and quilts in the window seat and found a photo album wrapped in an old newspaper. She took it out and carried it over to the rocker, where she sat down, opening it. The first three pages were filled with black and white photographs of Dr. and Mrs. DeVoss as young people, with a Florida background, alternating with other scenery, some of it apparently in the Alps. On page five a child appeared, first held by a nurse, its hands closed into fists. It had to be Pete. She wondered why this album had been kept here at Greenworld and was suddenly surprised, realizing she had never before seen photographs of Pete as a young boy growing up. Of course six months of marriage together is not very long. Only a limited number of things could be done. And with Pete flying most of the time, the bed was the most important furniture when he was home. Still, it seemed a bit strange, in retrospect.

She turned the two-dimensional time machine and studied Pete taking his first steps, Pete on his first tricycle, Pete going off to school, and Pete on a bicycle, always grinning—always looking into the camera, that half serious, half teasing look in his eyes as though he knew some joke on the world no one else was aware of. The photographs ran out when he was around fourteen. In the last one, he was wearing lederhosen, his arm in a sling. Some of the muscles she had felt against her softer flesh could already be seen. His blond hair spilled over the edge of his eyebrows, and he looked directly into the camera, directly into her eyes with a persistent stare, the old grin gone, as though the broken arm, the fall from an Austrian mountain side, had somehow revealed to him the fact that he had only eighteen more years to walk the green earth.

Anna turned the last page and stared curiously at the large photograph which had been taped faced-down to the inside surface of the album cover. Several small pieces of Scotch tape held it in place. She wondered what could possibly be in the photo. Whatever it was, Mrs. DeVoss had not wanted it seen by a casual observer, yet had not wished to destroy it. Using her fingernails, she peeled very slowly at the tape until it came loose without tearing the surface to which it adhered. Then she stopped, feeling guilty. But she knew that was not going to discourage her, and she knew that soon, in the next few minutes or half hour, she would have overcome it. Oh, hell, she thought, why put it off? She worked more rapidly with the strips of tape, still succeeding in removing them intact. She turned the photograph over and stared at it. It was a color print of Maud DeVoss as a young woman—Maud DeVoss gloriously naked.

And she was beautiful. Long auburn hair

flowed down across her shoulders and down her back, out of sight, to her waist. Her face was without blemish, the wrinkles of age concealed far below the surface of the creamy white skin. There was a provocative, daring look about her half-closed eyes and open lips, as though she invited all the men in the world to visit her. Anna thought she had seen that expression on the face of Jean Harlow, in an old movie magazine she had thumbed through somewhere. But the love goddess in this photograph did not recline. She stood with her back to Butterfly Falls, her right knee crooked, her arms hanging loosely. In the background, Butterfly Falls was suspended in time, silent forever, holding still with the eternal state of the beautiful woman. Anna tried to visualize Dr. DeVoss holding the camera and imagine what he was thinking as he laughed at his seductive wife. She wondered if perhaps in a glimmer of perception, he had looked beneath that white skin and that flowing hair to glimpse the wrinkles shining against the bones beneath.

Suddenly she was very sad. She looked down at her own white arm and shuddered. Carefully, she taped the photograph back in place, rewrapped the album, and returned it to its place beneath the blankets. Afterwards, she took off her clothes and entered the bathroom, closing the door. She posed before the full-length mirror. Her body was as it had been the last time she looked. The fine flesh, all of her was the same. She really was pretty! She could see no shadow lines of age, no ugly shadows against her white bones. She leaned closer and examined her face, stretching the skin with her fingertips. It was still young and unblemished. She inhabited the same world as the photograph of Maud DeVoss, but her world was ticking toward the world Mrs. DeVoss now occupied. She suddenly felt time pressing on her like a stream of invisible sand pouring down on her from above. She sighed and returned to her bedroom, dressing again.

The next Saturday was cold and cloudy, a cold breeze tousling the leaves outside the cabin. During the morning, dressed in a cardigan sweater and slacks, Anna drove to Boone to shop at a supermarket. It was not good weather for mountain tourism. Nevertheless, the narrow roads were as busy as a line of ants with lowlanders coming up for the weekend. Most of the license plates were local, although there were a few from adjacent states and an occasional one from farther away. Few of them were from Florida, she noted. Most of the Florida summer citizens had already begun their seasonal sojourn, and it was a bit early in the morning and much too cool for them to be abroad.

On the way home, Anna stopped at Sparr's Store for some needles and thread, which took only a few minutes. While she was waiting for the storekeeper to get the purchase from the ancient showcase, she listened to the two old-timers who were huddled close to the cold stove.

"Yep, hit's snowed in this county in ever month but July," one of them stated.

"Yeah," the other agreed, "we's bound to have a frost this year in August. You mark my word and set it down. The signs is right."

"Hit wouldn't s'prise me a-tall," the first agreed.

As Anna drove away from the store, she tried to conceive of snow in June and frost in August. It taxed her imagination. She shivered and laughed, wondering whether she could endure one cold winter up here above three thousand feet, when the chill factor was sometimes twenty below. Winter was not for her. Summer was beautiful here, but winter at some lower, warmer altitude was her idea of living sanely.

In the early afternoon there was a knock at the cabin door. Anna crossed the floor, a bit relieved because she expected it to be Jay Webber. She had seen him only once since her quick look at him at the Singing. He had come by briefly on Tuesday to deliver a letter from Maud DeVoss. (Her sister was resting easier, but she had decided not to return to the mountains just now.) The truth was, Anna was a little lonely and eager to see Jay. Perhaps they could go on a short horseback ride or something. The trouble was that it was Saturday, and she knew it. She had always been loneliest on Saturdays during her six years alone because it had been on the weekends that she was able to spend the most time with Pete, and they usually went out on Saturday nights.

She opened the door, smiling, but felt the elastic of her facial tissue slip back into neutral, which must have registered her disappointment. Anyway, the bright smile on Beatrice Wayne's face faded.

"Hi!" she said brightly. "Remember me?"

"Sure. Mrs. Wayne—Beatrice. Do come in."

Beatrice Wayne entered, and Anna closed the door. "It's a bit chilly today," her visitor said.

"Yes. If it keeps on with this rain and cold, they'll probably have frost here in August."

Beatrice laughed. "You're kidding. It's not possible."

"Oh, its quite possible," Anna argued. "Have a seat." She took one of the stuffed chairs near the fireplace and Beatrice Wayne sat in another.

"I'll tell you one thing," Beatrice asserted, hugging herself and pretending to shiver, "it frosts up here two nights in a row, and the Wayne family is heading back for sunny Florida."

"Could I get you a drink?" Anna asked. "Or perhaps some hot tea?"

"Hot tea would hit the spot, thanks."

Anna got up and went over to put water on a burner, then prepared tea cups. Beatrice Wayne told her she had walked all the way from her house through the woods, and she complained about the distance. "If you just had a telephone, I could have called you," she continued. "I just could not live without a telephone. Of course, I've been planning to visit you. I would have driven over if I had remembered how darn far it was."

"Didn't you ever walk over when the DeVosses were here?"

"Oh, many times. But I was a kid then, mostly. I had good wind. Besides—"

She stopped there. Anna wondered if the *besides* had anything to do with Pete. She carried the cups of tea back to her guest, who took one of them. Anna sat back down, then sipped the hot, lemony brew.

"Well, now, how did you like Mark Grunwald?" Beatrice asked, looking into her tea.

Anna stopped, her cup halfway to her mouth. She would have bet her old pantyhose that was the reason for the visit. For a moment she resented it, then thought, who cares? It was not that important. "Oh, okay, I guess. He's a real gentleman of the world."

"He's considered quite a catch by the summer people." Beatrice caught her eyes briefly, then looked away.

"For whom?"

"For whom!" Anna's guest laughed. "For any single woman that can get him." She hesitated. "Or any woman, for that matter. It's not a complicated matter anymore to become single."

"No," Anna agreed. "All a woman has to do is to have a husband who gets killed."

"Oh, honey, I'm sorry." She reached over and patted Anna's arm, spilling some of her tea. "I didn't intend to bring back memories. I was just kidding, naturally."

"No offense. I just stated it as a fact."

"Did—did you get along with Mark all right? He wouldn't talk about it to me."

"Why should he?" Anna had not meant to sound so firm.

"Oh, don't misunderstand me." She reached out to pat Anna's arm again, but she moved it before Beatrice could slop any of her tea onto her knees. "I was talking with him, and he brought the subject up himself. He just said how very pretty you are and how he wished he could see more of you. I mean be with you more."

"That was sweet of him."

"*Did* you-all have fun?" Beatrice Wayne hesitated. "I mean—"

"Do you mean, did we go to bed?" Anna asked politely. "If so, the answer is no, we didn't."

"Oh, Anna, you *know* I didn't mean that, really," she protested. "You *know* I wouldn't ask you anything like that."

"Well, just in case you are curious, we didn't."

"Oh, I could have guessed that." Beatrice reached out to touch her again, then withdrew her hand. "What I really came over here for—I mean aside from a neighborly visit—was to ask you over to play bridge tonight. My husband's brother is up from Orlando for a week, and we—George and I—thought it might be good for both of you to socialize a little. I mean you and Phil, my brother-in-law."

"I would be glad to come over. But bridge—don't you remember when I met you at the lodge, I told you I don't play bridge?"

"Oh, dear!" Beatrice Wayne looked incredulous. "Don't play bridge! Well, I declare. Well, what do you play?"

Anna managed a narrow little smile. "I'm a fairly good poker player."

"Poker! I mean poker?" Anna's guest nodded, her face twisted in puzzlement.

"My husband was a Navy jet pilot. He thought bridge was a game to keep the hands busy while women gossiped."

"Yes. Well, I suppose we could play a little poker. That would be fun, I suppose."

"It's settled then. What time should I come over?"

"Oh, I'll send Phil after you. We're invited to a little reception at the lodge earlier in the evening. How would eight-thirtyish be?"

"Eight-thirtyish will suit me fine," Anna said. "But I insist, I'll just come on over. I can't stay late, though. This mountain air gets to me. I usually retire early."

"That'll be fine, then." Beatrice Wayne stood up. "We'll be expecting you around eight-thirty."

Anna started to offer her a ride back to her cabin, but changed her mind. "See you then," she said, as she moved to open the door.

Some little niggling quirk at the back of her mind insisted that Anna walk to the Wayne cabin rather than drive. Although twilight beneath the forest roof preceded the setting of the sun, the old path between the summer homes was easy to follow. Anna wondered how many times young Pete DeVoss had walked this way to play with prissy little Beatrice Paulson, and felt a sharp little *ping!* of jealousy explode somewhere in the uncharted regions of her mind. Once, she stopped to watch five or six wee folk doing a square dance circle in the gloom beneath a holly tree, but when she blinked, they had vanished. She frowned in disappointment and continued her walk, her red pantsuit a shadow among shadows. Fireflies began exploding among the trees like the birth and death of distant stars.

"Oh, you walked!" Beatrice Wayne commented, when she opened the door.

"Yes," Anna said. "It was not all that far. Only a few hundred yards."

Phil Wayne was a big, blond man, perhaps twenty-five. Within two minutes after the game had started, Anna was made aware of the fact that he was a vice-president of one of the five Wayne banks in central and north Florida. Anna did not ask, but she was certain the banks were family enterprises, probably established by Father or Grandfather Wayne. How else could a man not long out of college become the vice-president of a bank? He wore a white sport shirt open almost to his navel, displaying his deeply tanned, almost hairless chest. He wore a smile as white as his shirt, and his hair, almost to his collar, any female would have envied. He was not feminine, though. He was quick to let her know he had been a linebacker at Florida State and a letterman in tennis. Did she play tennis? Did she play golf? He had another week's vacation. He would have to try her out next week if her calendar was not too full. Perhaps they could borrow the Webbers' horses and go for a ride. He knew some bridle paths leading to beautiful scenery—like Holy Rood Rock—since he had ridden with that local fellow (What was his name? Oh, yes, Jay—Jay Webber) last summer. A peckerwood, but a darn considerate chap. Anna felt her nape bristling and started to retort, then dropped it. After all, who was this Florida cracker? Jay did not need her to defend him.

Although her drinks had relaxed her and subdued her impatience, Anna was restless. The game, draw poker, was mostly slipshod and quiet except for the occasional chatter from Beatrice or the recreational autobiography of Phil, who drove a Corvette, flew the bank's Beechcraft, owned a twin-engine cabin cruiser, water skied, snow skied, piloted a racing boat, and was taking lessons to fly the company helicopter. Anna found herself wondering when in hell he found the time to play vice-president of a bank. She wondered how he and silent George could have come from the same tree, unless their mother had only one tongue to go around and Phil inherited it. Beatrice had to interpret George's silence and occasional grunts for Anna. Phil apparently knew the language.

"Summer is nothing up here for sports," Phil was saying. "You ought to come up here in the winter. They've got six or seven ski resorts around here. A couple of them have runs that are fairly challenging. Have you ever skied, Anna?"

Anna nodded, studying her hand. "On the Chesapeake Bay."

"No! I mean real skiing—snow skiing." He leaned toward her, smiling.

"The deepest snow I ever saw was about three inches," she said. "It closed Norfolk down for three days."

"Well, you ought to come back up here in January and February." Phil leaned forward against the table, plunging down a slope into the cold wind. "You'd love to ski. I could teach you in no time. I belong to the Ski Patrol."

"I just knew you did," Anna nodded solemnly. "I would have bet you were a Ski Patrolman."

"Draw, again," Beatrice announced. It was dealer's choice. "Deuces and one-eyed Jacks are wild."

"Jesus, Sis," Phil complained, "why don't you just make the whole deck wild?"

"Are you kidding?" Beatrice argued. "That would take all chance out of the game."

Anna had to admit that Phil Wayne was a bright kid, even when talking. As the evening progressed, more and more of the coins accumulated in front of him. By eleven, Anna was out of chips, including two dollars extra she had brought along, a total of five dollars and twenty cents. But of more importance to her, she was weary of the game, weary of the Waynes, and under the influence of the cool mountain air, was too sleepy to pretend any longer. She wanted to be alone.

The second after she excused herself for the evening, Anna realized where she had made her mistake—by walking to the Wayne cabin instead of driving. Phil Wayne had the answer. "Oh, I'll drive you home. It's too far to walk in the dark. I must. I insist." Anna knew he would. She was a bit tipsy from the drinks, and anyway, she did not feel like arguing. Anna was afraid for a moment he would insist on carrying her to his car.

He almost lifted her into the bucket seat of the low-swung vehicle, then vaulted the hood toward the driver's side. In a moment they were out of the yard and heading up the Ridge Road, Phil Wayne talking, talking, talking. What a way to spend a Saturday evening, she thought. Way ahead, the

Webber farmhouse was a dark, rectangular mass against a lighter sky. She wondered if Jay were asleep or somewhere with the redhead she had seen him with at the Singing. She felt a little lurch of regret at the possibility, but it passed quickly.

Phil Wayne did not touch her except to help her out of the car. When she stumbled on the front steps, he grabbed her left arm, steadying her, then let her go. Damn, but she was tight, tighter than she realized or had intended, probably because she had eaten very little all day. She groped for the keyhole, found it, inserted the key, and the door swung inward.

It was at that moment Phil Wayne touched her. He seized her in his arms, drew her to him, and found her mouth with his. Anna started to shove him away, then thought better. Perhaps a quick kiss would satisfy him and send him home more quickly. But he had other ideas. For a moment Anna's mind whirled away toward alcoholic indiscretion.

He removed his mouth from hers. "I just knew you would be like this," he panted. "Yes. Yes. I knew you would."

Promise you'll wait till I return.

Anna went tense. "Like what?"

"Warm," he whispered. "Exciting!"

"I'm not like that at all," she stated, pushing at him. "Knock it off! That's enough, buster."

But she could not budge his bulk. She braced a

forearm against his chest and shoved, but it only moved her backward tighter against the wall, where he trapped her. All of a sudden his closeness repelled her. She did not want him close to her. The cracker called Jay a peckerwood. Wish he were here. Let him go back to the Sunshine State and brag to his friends at the bank—

"Come on, beautiful," he crooned in her ear. "You know you don't want to fight me."

With her right hand, Anna tried to reach his face with her fingernails, but he caught her wrist with his left hand. Her left hand was trapped behind her against the wall.

Relax a moment, the ghost voice whispered deep in her brain. *Remember what I taught you. Relax, then when he relaxes, you know what to do.*

The short hair bristled on the nape of her neck. She could feel the blood draining from her face, but briefly she felt more secure with the living flesh of Phil Wayne close to her. But for only a moment. Then she relaxed and Phil Wayne placed his arms back around her. She pushed him gently, and he moved backward just enough.

Abruptly, her right knee flashed upward and caught him in the crotch. He bellowed a hoarse, coughing groan and doubled over, clutching himself with both hands. She slipped from between him and the wall, darted through the doorway, and shoved the cabin door closed. She stood there in the dark panting, terrified that he would be intoxicated enough and stupid enough to break into the cabin and attack her again. She remembered Pete's advice clearly now. "Women have no pain equivalent," he had laughed.

Her breathing had slowed to normal, and her heart had quieted when she heard the engine of the Corvette come to life. She smiled a tight smile of relief and crossed the cabin to her bedroom, turning on the light.

Afterwards, she stood under a hot shower for half an hour, almost scalding herself clean.

Chapter X

She sat on a mossy rock somewhere in the forest watching the wee folk square-dancing. She did not see any musicians, but the little people, in their white and black pilgrim clothes, danced wildly, like Breughel's peasants, their heads thrown back, silent laughter ringing toward the sky. Suddenly the dancing stopped and the wee folk whirled to face her, looking beyond her, their faces warped by fear. Only a moment they stood frozen in their tracks. Then they whirled and fled beneath some healalls.

Anna started to turn and look behind her, but she was too late. A powerful hand seized her right arm, whirled her onto her back. She felt a hairy chest flatten her and coarse hair cutting into her skin like steel wool. Both her wrists were grasped now. She tried to rear up, but was pressed back. She could think of no defense that Pete had taught her. She was half terrified and half fascinated. She opened her eyes and stared upward. The face was indistinct, but the kinky hair and beard were in vague silhouette against the starry sky and seemed familiar. The thick neck which came down to press against her face had a familiar smell, one remembered from a long time ago. She opened her mouth to plead, but could not speak.

Her eyes were open now, and she was staring at the shadowy ceiling above the bed. The weight was gone from her chest, but she thought she could still smell a faint musk in the room. She tossed her head to the side. The window was open, but the screen was closed and latched.

She heard a noise at the window. Tilting her head again, she stared in that direction. She thought she saw a shadowy silhouette against the outer darkness. She whirled to the edge of the bed, lifting the lid of the window seat and groping downward inside it. She found the button that rang the bell in the Webber house. Her hand relaxed and she stared back at the window, squinting. There was nothing there. Of course there was not.

She started to withdraw her hand, hesitated. All she had to do was press the button. Her finger stiffened on it. In ten minutes or less, perhaps only five, Jay would be there inside the house. Why had she not been tempted before? Was it because fantasies seemed more possible, more acceptable in the middle of the night, when she usually slept? Anyway, she was unafraid for the present.

She removed her hand from inside the box and let the lid fall. Suddenly she was chilly. Reaching down, she pulled the sheet and blanket over herself, curled into a tight spiral, and smiled in comfort. She felt good through and through. Gad, but the bed was comfortable. She went back to sleep, still smiling.

Anna DeVoss sat at the large oval table in the Webber combination kitchen-dining room, a room large enough to hold a dance in, she thought. Around ten o'clock that morning she had heard the roar of Jay's Scout outside the cabin. He had come with the invitation from his mother to a Fourth of July dinner (a noon meal to Mrs. Webber), and Anna had been happy to accept. Independence Day was warm and hazy, but not muggy here in the mountains. Jay had shown her about the farm, the granary, the small greenhouse, the smokehouse, and the stone basement beneath the kitchen area, where Burley tobacco was cured.

Now, the four of them ate—Jay, Anna, Hilda, and Mrs. Webber, who did most of the talking. It was as though she had saved her word-hoard during the quiet days of the working week, Anna thought, and spent it on whoever there was to listen on weekends and holidays. Her reddish gray-streaked hair was combed back and wound into a tight bun at the nape of her neck. Wearing her navy-blue Sunday dress, Mrs. Webber did not appear to Anna to be a hard working farm woman until she looked at the older woman's hands, cracked and calloused as any man's who has spent a lifetime in the fields.

Anna's glance flickered to Hilda, beside her mother. She sat in her chair as prim as a first-year student in a boarding school. Her red dress, patterned with white daisies, was neatly laundered, and her long hair swept down her back, held in order behind, Anna had noticed earlier, by a silver barrette. Her whole attention was on her food and the ritual of eating it, lifting each forkful slowly and placing it in her mouth as carefully as though she expected it to burn her. She glanced at Anna now and then, but mostly, she practiced a pantomime she had been carefully rehearsed in for a long time. Wearing what seemed to be the same faded jeans and sleeveless blue sports shirt, Jay sat across from Anna. Now and then their eyes would meet, like a tentative fingertip-to-fingertip touch by two people in a dark room. At those times, a ripple of laugh wrinkles would appear about his eyes, hedged in by hairline and beard, but Anna could not tell whether they were from amusement or pleasure. He ate methodically as though counting the calories, pausing now and then to stare through the window beyond Anna, his mind apparently far away.

"I got seven younguns," Mrs. Webber was saying. "There's Hilder and Jay, my youngst'uns. Then there's Goldie and Ruth and Maybell, living here and yander." She grinned. "Already fetched me eight grandchildrens. Then I got two older boys, Abe and Sandy. They's both off yander in Dee-troit and Denver. Couldn't neither of 'em abide working on the farm. That's why Jay's got to manage things—"

"Mamma!" Jay protested.

Martha Webber laughed. "Jay don't take to me talkin about him to nobody. He's my youngun that's most inside hisself. He's my brightest 'un, too." She chuckled. "Although he don't behave like it most of the time."

Jay Webber grinned and caught Anna's eye. "Mamma thinks I'm bright because I get things done without killing myself working at it."

"No, I don't think no sech a thing," his mother argued. "That's the part I think is lazy. Hard work is good for soul and body."

"Mamma, may I be excused to go to the bathroom, please?" Hilda Webber asked.

"Sure, honey. Be careful to flush the toilet, now, and wash your hands before you come back to the table."

"Yes, Mamma." The girl left, disappearing through the doorway to Anna's left, leading to the main part of the house.

The food was delicious. The main dish was fried chicken, but the vegetables appealed to Anna's taste the most. There were string beans seasoned with pork, and mashed potatoes. There was also a dish she had never tasted before, leaf lettuce covered with sliced spring onions, wilted by pouring some hot bacon grease over them. This early in the summer, leaf lettuce and spring onions were about the only vegetables the garden produced here in the mountains, Mrs. Webber had told her earlier, especially if the season is late. There were sliced tomatoes, tasty and tart, not like the plastic` blobs she was able to buy in the supermarket, picked and shipped green. Anna loved home-grown, vine-ripened tomatoes.

"I didn't think tomatoes were ripe up here in the mountains yet," she said. "They are delicious."

"That's one of the reasons I think Jay's smart," Martha Webber grinned. "He tuck over one of my greenhouses I use for flowers (she pronounced it *flairs*) and growed some early tomatoes in there. Uses jest manure and woods mulch to feed'em. They are good, aint't they?"

"It was a simple job," Jay said. "That's the way I'm raising everything in the garden down at Riverglade."

"Now, honey, you know better'n that," Mrs. Webber said firmly. "Get back to your room and get your dress back on."

Anna turned her head. Hilda stood in the doorway, naked except for her panties. "But, Mamma, I wet my dress."

Anna's eyes shifted to Jay, as he turned to look at his sister. "Hilda, baby, we have company," he said. "Please! Go back and put a dress on."

"Get you another clean frock out of your dresser drawer," Martha Webber said. "Now you know you mustn't come in here like that."

"All right, Mamma." The girl turned around and disappeared back through the doorway. Anna studied Martha Webber covertly and envied her children their mother.

"Jay will excuse me if I tell you he don't like running the farm much," Mrs. Webber said. "After J.W. passed on, they wasn't nobody else to manage. I couldn't. We let the backer allotment out to a tenant farmer, but we got a share. Mack Jones is honest enough, but Burley backer needs to be tuck care of like a sick baby. Jay knows how it's got to be done, and so he manages it. If he had his druthers, he'd druther not do much of anything but raise a garden and a few acres of other stuff."

"After a man has worked himself to death," Jay protested, "all he's got to show for it is a hole in the ground and property left for his kin to fight over."

"They won't be no fightin over this here farm," his mother argued.

"That's because Dad was smarter than most farmers. He made plans for his land."

"Mountain lands is breakin up," Martha Webber explained to Anna. "This generation cares but little or nothin about real farmin. Most of 'em are leaving home for factories and professions, them that ain't already left. They was a time when everbody that could manage it, around here, sent their girls to Appalachian State Teachers College— it's a university now, but it was a fine teachers college for year upon year. Then the girls would marry some local boy, and they'd farm and have a good income from her a-teachin in a nearby school and her man a-runnin the farm. But things has changed. Boys and girls both are a-goin to the university, here and way off yander, some'ers, and the land is gettin broke apart into sections and lots for them rich lowlanders to invest in or so's they can spend the summers up here where it's cool at. And they ain't no more plan to the developin and buildin than a house on fire. Big old mansions and scabby trailers are a settin next door to one another like a frog in a flower garden."

"Yet there's no other place worth living, at least for me," Jay said. "You couldn't pay me to leave these mountains anymore."

"But don't you get bored up here sometimes?" Anna was arguing with him. She felt it was a point she needed to make. "I mean, this summer so far has been wonderful for me, different. But isn't that because it's a new experience? Deep down, I feel restless, quite often, as though—" She was thoughtful for a few seconds—"as though I wanted to go home and couldn't remember where home is."

"You're becoming one of us," Jay laughed. "If you weren't, you'd remember where your home is."

Anna opened her mouth to deny what he had said, then thought better. After all, there was nothing to protest against, even though she was sure what he had said was untrue.

Chapter XI

Jay Webber had invited Anna to attend the nineteenth annual Highland Games and Gathering of the Scottish Clans, on Saturday, July 13, at McRae Meadows, under Grandfather Mountain, where she had attended alone the "Singing on the Mountain." The event was to last two days, Saturday and Sunday, but Jay was chiefly interested in the track and field competition, which took place on Saturday. He asked her to be ready by 6:00 A.M. so they could escape the frustrating traffic, and Anna, remembering her experience at the Singing, agreed. It was already daylight as they sped along the winding highway toward Linville in Jay's Scout, but a sky full of woolly fog hung a few hundred feet above the treetops, canceling out sunrise or any other means of telling direction. Grandfather Mountain was buried from below his chin upward, including Calloway Peak, his nose, the highest elevation in the Blue Ridge Chain.

Jay's concession to family tradition and the MacTavish Clan (actually a family of the Campbell Clan) was a pair of trousers made of MacTavish tartan—a plaid with a red background, lines of light blue and black running through it. His shirt was a non-symbolic light blue pullover. Anna wore a Campbell tartan scarf about her head, which Mrs. Webber had supplied. Jay had not attended the gathering in more than five years, he told her. In his late teens and early twenties he had worn the whole regalia: kilt, sporran, tam, everything; but he had lost interest in any kind of group identity, Anna gathered from what he did not say. She also sensed that his main reason for attending today was that he thought she might find it interesting.

"The guest of honor this year is from Clan Malcolm, Argyll, Scotland," Jay explained, as he made the last turn at the Linville traffic light and headed toward Grandfather Mountain on 221. "The chief of a clan is invited from Scotland each year to renew the kinship between American and native clansmen. Some of the games are traditional Scottish contests, and some, like the track and jumping events, are universal. It was a good idea to start with, a real celebration of tradition, but I'm afraid it's getting too polluted by tourists."

"Why is the gathering here?" Anna asked. "I mean, why not somewhere else?"

"The Carolina mountains are full of descendants of Scottish immigrants." They were climbing now under a canopy of green foliage, swinging from curve to curve with the rhythm of a roller coaster, up the west side of the Blue Ridge. "Many refugees of the Jacobean troubles ended up here, because it was so much like the highlands, I'm sure. Some of the most common names are McRae, McNeal, McGee, McLeod, MacTavish, Scott, Ross, MacLeon, Davidson, Hay, Witherspoon (originally Wotherspoon), and so on. It's ironic that many of them are really humble farmers or low-income families who ignore their heritage and would never consider going to the trouble of coming to one of these gatherings, up here. Yet most of them I'm talking about have a greater family right to wear the tartan than most of those who will be here today, pretenders who are only indirectly connected to a Scottish clan."

"I suppose it's like you said earlier: some people feel a need to belong somewhere special. Perhaps they are ordinary, which I don't mean to be a criticism, and any kind of relationship to a proud heritage like the Scots have gives them a feeling of importance."

Jay nodded his head thoughtfully, but Anna was not sure whether he actually heard what she had said. He was once again off in his own little universe, leaving his flesh beside her.

They encountered no other vehicle on the climb to McRae Meadows, but when they arrived, they discovered a small city had preceded them. The grassy area on the right side of the highway was filled with campers, trailers, and cars around its margin, people who had arrived the day before. On the left side of the road, campers and cars stretched from sight in the cleared areas beneath the trees and in the grass along the edge of the vast upland meadow. Jay pulled into the entrance to the grounds, backed around, and parked on the grassy shoulder of the highway, with a light pole a few feet behind him, giving him enough space to back up and escape if someone should park too close to his front bumper. They sat in the car for a while drinking coffee from a thermos bottle Jay had brought, listening to a radio station in Morganton, hardly hearing it and saying very little.

Shortly after they parked, other vehicles began to arrive but they were infrequent, this early, and had little trouble finding a parking place. Most of them drove directly up the lane, directed by an attendant with a walkie-talkie, and into the lower area of McRae Meadows, where they would be stuck without escape until the day's activities were over and they had to creep in line out of the area. At eight o'clock, Anna and Jay left the Scout. Jay bought tickets at three dollars each for the first day, and they walked up the forest lane towards the meadow. Anna noted as they passed them, cars and campers from many states, several from as far away as Michigan and Canada.

Already, tourists and fourth and fifth-generation American Scotsmen were beginning to wander about the huge field. A stocky couple in kilts, hose, and tams waddled past Anna and Jay, holding hands. Both had long hair and both had a sturdy walk, making it difficult to tell which was the male and which the female. Jay argued that the man was on the right because the rear of the other one rotated a bit farther with each step. They got scrambled eggs, ham, biscuits and coffee in cardboard containers at a stand and sat down on a rock to eat. Anna's eyelids were heavy and grainy. She felt like stretching out on the grass and going back to sleep.

At nine, the sun broke through the rising fog as though a clock had been set for that moment. Tourists were beginning to pour into the lower half of the meadow now, streaming down the lanes between parked vehicles. Canvas kiosks were opening up, stretched along the middle of the meadow, offering everything for sale Scottish and a great deal that was not. They moved from stand to stand, examining the goods and their prices. Clan tartan kilts, little more than wraparounds, sold for $45 to $60. Tartan ties were $5 to $10, depending on their width. There was a variety of caps, tams, scarfs, sporrans, belts, socks, and other clothing. There was bolt upon bolt of tartan fabric. One could buy clan books, clan maps, family crests, ashtrays, cups, plates, banners, and badges which read "Kiss me, I'm Scottish" or "Scotland Forever." There were also expensive jewelry and junk jewelry—the sort that tourists revel in. One kiosk specialized in Scottish food, including short bread and haggis—lamb, seasoning, and oatmeal stuffed into a lamb's stomach.

They stopped to watch an old white-haired

gentleman hobble by dressed in expensive Scottish attire, sporran hair dangling far down between his bowed legs. He walked painfully by using one of those S-curved, knotty "hoot mon" canes Anna had seen in pictures.

"Old Great-grandpa Abe MacTavish would kick these stands down, if he could see them," Jay muttered. "Money changers in the temple of tradition."

"But the goods are authentic, aren't they?"

"Yes, a hell of a lot more authentic than the Cherokee tomahawks and headdresses made in Formosia you'll find in the southwestern part of the state, around Cherokee. At least it was like that a few years ago." He stopped suddenly and turned, waving with the back of his hand toward the milling, elbowing throng around them, as if attempting to part the Red Sea with a gesture. "But these people, eighty percent of them, are descendants of immigrants from everywhere but Scotland. There's something phony about selling ancestral symbols to *aliens,* if I can use that word. And even I've got to go back three generations to find pure Scot blood."

"It's the publicity," Anna said. "I bet you could have a gathering of orangutangs and write it up in papers or put it on TV, and you would have thousands of summer tourists who would come, claiming a distant ancestor was an orangutang chief."

Jay Webber stared at her, a strange look in his

eyes, his mouth grim. Suddenly he burst out laughing and whacked her on her arm, stinging her. "You know, I think there's hope for you yet."

Anna resented the pain briefly, but let it pass. She remembered Pete had said once that if you had a brown-nosing contest, and advertised it, you would get a stadium full of long noses from everywhere. She started to tell Jay, but thought better. That was something that belonged to her and her husband.

Jay escorted her through the gate between the lines of kiosks and out into the upper half of the meadow, the center of which was dominated by an official quarter-mile oval track around a grassy field, where high-jump, broad-jump, pole vault, and shot-put areas could be seen. The hillside to the left was terraced and offered tiers on which spectators had already gathered, sitting in folding chairs or on spread blankets. Jay and Anna sat in the grass on the upper tier to the right of the reviewing stand, a platform with a canvas roof, the microphone already manned by someone who called himself the Field Marshal.

"Traffic is backed up all the way to Linville, two miles," the Field Marshal announced. Anna looked at her watch. It was 9:45. He had said it as though it were some kind of record, perhaps better than last season, when the traffic did not reach that mark until later in the day.

She started to call Jay's attention to the time,

when the microphone came alive again. "Will the owner of the Buick station wagon blocking the driveway into the field please move it?" the voice requested. "Otherwise, it will be towed away at your expense."

"I be damned! Would you believe that?" Jay commented.

"He wanted to park close," Anna replied. "The driveway was obviously the only space in three miles of here he could get his little old Buick wagon in. He's a citizen. He's got rights."

Jay laughed. "You wouldn't believe that anyone, I mean *anyone,* would be that stupid, would you? Now he, or she, is going to lose twice as much time moving as he would have lost parking sensibly in the first place."

"That's democracy, Jay. You are free to be bright, mediocre, or stupid. Everyone can't be bright."

On two platforms down on the athletic field, children were doing the Highland Fling. They appeared to be all girls, but a boy would have been hard to spot from that distance, in a kilt and wearing long hair. The strident skirl of a bagpipe filled the air like the protest of a giant insect caught in a web, as bonnie lassies, from four feet to five feet, ten inches tall did their Scottish ballet, most of the motion vertical. Although there was a monotony to the repetition of the steps, Anna could see a wild grace in the dance and felt her nape prickle at the music. For a brief few seconds, she understood how warriors in kilts, their bottoms bare, could follow that music into battle, called by the enemy the Ladies from Hell.

"Did you know," Jay asked, "that the typical mountain fiddle music was originally an attempt to imitate the sound of the bagpipe?"

"No, I didn't know that," Anna said. "Did you know it?"

Jay chuckled. "You blasé smarty! No, I didn't know it, but I have been told that the Scottish immigrants to these mountains invented mountain fiddling because they missed bagpipe music. I was not told why they didn't bring bagpipes with them."

"You anticipated my question."

"I'm getting to know you," he sang off key.

They ate a production-line lunch and watched athletic competition in the afternoon. By one o'clock the grounds surrounding the field were so thick with spectators it was difficult to walk in any direction. The huge boulders along the upper edge of the meadows were so crowded, Anna was reminded of sunning seals on a rocky shore. The track and field events were sanctioned by the AAU, Jay explained, and any record set would be an official one. But as it turned out, only local track records were broken. Anna was not impressed, nor was Jay. Had it not been for the atmosphere and the setting, she would just as soon have been back at the cabin reading a book. The mile and two-mile runs were very slow, compared to world records. The hundred-yard dash was exciting only because it was explosive.

Anna found the caber toss the most interesting event because it was the most alien to her experience. The caber was a twenty-foot log which weighed from a hundred to a hundred forty pounds. The contestant picked it up from the ground, keeping it as vertical as possible, lifting it with both hands beneath the small end, rushed forward and hurled it top end first. The point was to toss it end over end so that it fell in line with the run, and not the distance thrown. The sport originated from a method of building bridges in a hurry, Jay told her. The sheaf toss and the toss of the clach—stone strength—a large, smooth stone which weighed about fourteen pounds, were also interesting.

They missed the most unusual happening of the day when a man with a hang glider sailed from the chin of Grandfather Mountain, fifteen hundred feet to a golf course at the foot of the mountain. Someone told them about it later. Anna tried to relate the glider flight to the Highland Games, but somewhere there was a contradiction.

Late in the afternoon, before the masses of tourists got the same idea, Anna and Jay walked among the sprawling, standing, milling spectators, returning to the highway and Jay's Scout. As they drove back toward Linville, traffic was no problem, but the shoulder of the road on the right was a continuous line of parked vehicles.

"Can you imagine what it will be like when all those cars and campers start leaving McRae Meadows?" Anna asked, out of a long silence.

"Yes, I can." He looked at her, then back at the road. "That's why we're leaving now. These roads are not capable of handling this kind of traffic. Only four-lane roads could do it."

Imagine what four lanes would do to these mountains."

"That's our dilemma," he nodded.

Chapter XII

The week following the Highland Games, Jay Webber started coming by Anna's cabin almost every day, suggesting some activity. On Monday he drove her several miles the other side of Boone, to the old Winebarger mill. His stated reason for making the trip was to buy some fresh-ground buckwheat flour, but she was sure the real reason was to show her the old water mill. A faded, dark structure of weatherboarding and shingles, it towered beside a small stream whose water ran eternally down the flume and overshot the rusty waterwheel, turning it, unless a trap was opened, allowing the water to fall short, splashing on the rocks below. The mill was over eighty years old and now run by the grandson of the first miller.

Inside, the building was close and filled with a "mealy fragrance of the past," Anna thought. Always, with the wheel turning, the floor vibrated beneath her feet and the low rumble, along with the grating of meshing steel cogs, reminded her of an approaching avalanche of stones. All over the walls and beams, the names and addresses of customers from as far away as California and Maine were written in square script, along with the amount of meal or buckwheat flour to be mailed and the intervals at which orders were to be sent. Some of them were dated 1887, 1900, and 1906. Anna had the weird feeling that she would walk back out through the door she used earlier, when she entered the old mill, step up into a buggy, and ride off at a fast trot. And to her surprise she almost wished she could.

That night, Jay drove Anna out to Wisemans View, off Highway 181, and they sat for four hours staring at the dark bulk of Brown Mountain, trying to catch a glimmer of the ghostly Brown Mountain Lights, but all they saw were fireflies.

On Tuesday, Jay came by her cabin with the horses and a picnic lunch his mother had packed, suggesting that they ride up to Holy Rood Rock. They passed by the dark green lake of growing tobacco, through which a man, a woman, and several teenagers waded slowly, at work. Jay told her about Burley 21, suckering, cutworms, and aphids, but she did not follow it too well. Raising tobacco seemed like more trouble than running a dairy.

"That weed is a royal pain in the ankle," Jay swore. "And I'm getting fed up with it. It's like bottle-feeding a rattlesnake. It doesn't contribute a damn thing to mankind but trouble. I sometimes try to imagine the kind of vegetables you could grow with the same pampering."

Anna looked at him curiously. "What's the occasion for this sermon? I don't smoke, and I haven't seen you smoking."

Jay laughed brusquely. "I'm sorry. One of my sore points. As far as I personally am concerned, raising tobacco is immoral. Yet I'm trapped, at least for this year. I have to manage it for Mamma and Hilda. But Mom doesn't really need the money anymore."

They climbed halfway up Golgotha Mountain, following a winding bridle trail beneath tall oaks and poplars. Holy Rood Rock was far from symmetrical, but it was massive and intimidating. Anna stood beside her mount and stared up at it, subdued to silence, momentarily. Both vertical shaft and cross bar were of sedimentary rock, with strata easily visible in different shades of limestone and large fragments of quartz. The shaft, more than sixty feet tall, listed to the left. The right arm of the horizontal beam was shorter than the left, and the whole formation was tilted slightly from horizontal. Sometime in the dark geological past, Anna surmised, the two layers of rock had collided during earthquakes, had become fused, and millions of years of erosion had done the rest. It was the kind of cross a blind giant might have chiseled out, and for a moment a dark stone Christ three stories tall shimmered against it, before disappearing. A spring bubbled from the base of the cliff behind the cross and rushed down to the stone foundation, sweeping around both sides of the vertical shaft.

"Whoever drinks of that spring," Jay said quietly, "will live in extremely good health."

The spell was broken. Anna turned on him. "Aw, come on," she scoffed. "You don't really believe that crap!"

"That's the tradition," he said. "The Indians believed it. There's a Cherokee myth that de Soto worshipped here on his way through the Appalachians to the Mississippi and that he took some of the water with him.'

"If he did, the water didn't save him, did it?" She was thoughtful a moment. "Old Cortez would have crucified an Indian or two on it."

"The Cherokees called it Equa-nvya-asgaya, Big Rock Man." He hesitated. "There's a better tradition than the one about the water, though."

"Whoever eats a rock from beneath it will never have diarrhea?" Anna asked, smiling.

"No, smarty. Whoever is married beneath Holy Rood Rock will never separate."

Anna turned to look at him, another smart remark on the tip of her tongue. But Jay Webber was staring upward at the cross. And she did not want to change the expression on his face. "Are many couples married here?" she asked quietly.

"Not any more." He lowered his head and stared back across Holy Rood Valley, which lay below in haze like a land beneath a translucent lake. A generation ago they did. My parents were married here. Our generation doesn't believe in such magic. Besides, you can't get up here unless you walk or ride horseback. And I don't think many of the backpackers from outside even know about it."

"You know what's going to happen, don't you?"

"What?" He studied her face, eyes narrowed.

"One day soon, they'll build a road up here. Hamburger stands will spring up. There'll be a picnic ground. The tourists will come with their candy wrappers, paper plates, cans, and bottles, and there will be mass weddings under the cross, televised. And little plastic Holy Rood Rocks will sell at five dollars each. And the bride and groom who kiss the longest will get a gold-filled dishwasher."

Jay Webber laughed a scoffing little laugh. "You're a sardonic broad."

"I'm not a broad, Jay. I'm Anna. Remember?"

Reaching out, he took hold of her left arm, squeezing it, then let it go. "I'm sorry, Anna. I was kidding. But you're wrong about one thing—the tourists coming like that. This is one natural wonder that will never be corrupted."

"Why not? Have you ever seen the mess left behind in the stadium, after the lions have eaten the Christians?"

"Because of two unique men, Anna. My father and Dr. DeVoss bought over three hundred acres around the rock back when land was cheap. It belongs to Holy Rood Rock in perpetuity. No road can be built up here, not ever, unless America becomes a dictatorship."

"Well I'll be—I'll be—damned."

"Surprising, isn't it?" He took her by the arm and turned her to face him. "But don't be damned. Live in good health, my friend. Come on, let's drink."

On the way back from the rock, Jay took her over a three-mile loop, far to the southeast of the Webber farmhouse, through woods and fallow fields rich with wildflowers. Wherever it was possible, especially in fallow fields, he rode beside her and pointed out numerous flowers, describing them to her, especially those medicinal or edible. Some of them she had already looked up in the book back at the cabin, but she did not tell him. He explained that the purple-tufted healall, a mint, was once used in folk medicine for throat ailments. He pointed to the scarlet flame of oswego tea, or bee-balm, which lit up the corner of an old rail fence like a flame. Horse mint, he told her, was important for its leaves and not for its purple flowers. The leaves were used as a medicine for colic, and the mint oil was distilled from them for flavoring. There was something quietly frantic about Jay Webber's instructions. He reminded Anna of a professor trying to cover the last chapter of a textbook on the last day of the semester. She kept studying him covertly, but he hardly looked away from the plants he was describing.

The woolly-leaved mullen, or flannel-leaf, topped by a long, flowering stem, was used to make cough medicine, he told her. In a fallow meadow he said his father had once mowed for its wild hay, he pointed to a tall, leafy cluster of plants with frosty-pink crown flowers. "That's queen-of-the-meadow," he told Anna. "It's also called Joe-pye weed. People used to make a tonic of its roots for diarrhea." In a dark glade, they came upon an old stone chimney, a monument to some long-gone family, but grass and wildflowers and briars had covered any other signs that sorrow and laughter had once sat before the open fireplace. Nearby were several tall, thin plants with flowers so brilliantly blue they seemed to glow in the shadows of the briars and ragweeds. "Have you ever seen packages of coffee with *chicory added* printed on them?" Jay asked.

"I used to have a girl friend whose parents used it," she replied. "That coffee was cheaper than most, she told me."

"That's chicory." He pointed to the blue flowers. "That plant has a deep taproot, and it's dried up and ground, then mixed with coffee. It's supposed to make the coffee flavor better."

He pointed out to her Turk's cap, which reminded her of tiger lilies with a strong wind blowing the petals back; yellow clustered primrose; and acres of asters, whose blue or white blossoms reminded her of tiny daisies. Once, as they rode beside a mass of granite beneath bush-topped field pines, Jay dismounted and pulled a handful of glossy leaves from a mass of herbs growing along the edges of the rock. Small urn-shaped pinkish flowers dotted the bed of leaves. Jay thrust some of the leaves into his mouth and began to chew them, handing a cluster up to her. She hesitated, then followed his example. The flavor was strong and unmistakably wintergreen, like her favorite mint.

"That was teaberry plants," he said. "They're also called wintergreen by outsiders, for obvious reasons."

When they finally reached the DeVoss cabin, Anna dismounted and leaned for a moment against Blitzen. She was exhausted. Jay Webber was slumped in his saddle staring at his hands, which held the reins loosely. Anna walked in front of the mare and handed her reins up to him. He glanced down at her, took them, then stared across the top of Anna's head, out into the woods.

"Thanks for a nice day," she said. "I really enjoyed it."

Looking back down at her, he smiled. She had the impression he had talked so much about plants, he was too tired to respond. She started to turn away, then turned back, squinting up at him through her huge sunglasses. "And thanks for the informative botany lecture, Professor."

As he looked down at her, his mouth became narrow and straight between mustache and beard. His eyes narrowed. "I'd hoped you would get more out of it than information," he stated. He did not wait for her to answer but wheeled his mount and rode off up the driveway through the woods, leading Blitzen.

"Well, darn my hide!" Anna muttered, using a nicer version of an old Pete DeVoss expression. "I didn't aim to go and step on your bottom lip, neighbor."

Jay did not come by on Wednesday. When he drove up in his scout around 10:00 A.M. on Thursday, he gave no explanation of his activities the day before. And, as a matter of fact, there was no reason he should have, Anna reasoned. Hearing the engine, she hurried out onto the front deck as he parked in the bay beside her car. He got out, stretched, and grinned.

"Got any plans for today, tenderfoot?"

"I had intended to write a book and a couple of songs," Anna said. "But I can do that any time. What did you have in mind, big, white hunter?"

"I thought I'd take you up on the highest mountain in the promised land and show you all the kingdoms of the world."

"Your cluttered metaphor eludes me. Specifically, what is your proposition, expressed in basic English?"

"Would you, Anna DeVoss, like to go for a ride?"

"Let's go." She slammed the cabin door and ran down the steps, vaulting into the passenger side of the front seat.

Leaving the Holy Rood Valley, Jay turned left at the highway and headed toward Boone. He did not say much at first, but he glanced occasionally at her as though he wanted her to start a conversation. When he braked to a stop at the traffic light in Boone, at the intersection with U.S. 321, he leaned back and prodded her shoulder with an index finger.

"Five or six years ago," he said, "this was still a peaceful little mountain town, an ideal spot for the university here. Now, it's getting to be a tourist Mecca, in the worst sense of the term, at least from my viewpoint. The traffic problem is atrocious in the summer, and every ski season it's getting worse in the winter. Would you believe that people by the score come up here to ski without either snow tires or chains? You can see their cars strung out along the shoulders and in the ditches when they get caught by a sudden snowstorm. They even try to climb the mountain on worn tires in falling snow."

"Yes, I'd believe that," she said carefully. "It sounds like about par to me." She wondered if this was going to be another anti-tourist lecture and hoped there would be more to the ride than that.

With no traffic interfering, Jay turned right on the red light and headed south on 321. They were on a four-lane stretch, paralleled by shopping centers and both old and new businesses.

"Not long ago, say four years," Jay continued, "a long, grassy ridge lay to the left there, tapering to end at Boone Creek—see the bank growth? Look how flat it is now, from that clay bluff to the creek. Perfect terrain for that shopping center. In an amazingly short time bulldozers and backhoes dug that ridge away, rocks and all, and trucks hauled it across the highway and dumped it into the low area on our right. Now we have a flat plain bisected by the creek, which will soon be going into a culvert, underground. One of these days they're going to have the damndest flood here you ever saw.

"I miss the green ridge, but that doesn't bother me as much as the other digging still going on. What really bothers me is digging back into hillsides and ridges along the streets and roads, carving out notches to build in, leaving the clay banks and blasted rocks to distort the landscape. Many of those little old chain diners and dinky gift shops are built like that."

"If there's demand for such food and such dowdy doodads, what do you object to?" Anna asked. She understood what he was getting at, but thought a devil's advocate might create a dialogue instead of a monologue of just bitching.

"I object mostly because it's brash, two-bit, chrome-and-neon Americana. I simply object to that at its face value. If such building is permitted, then the builders should be forced to landscape the excavations—slant the banks and plant grass and shrubbery. The ticky-tacky tourist traps wouldn't look so atrocious with a bit of green around them."

"Whoa, man!" Anna held up her hand. "You're getting emotional. Keep it rational or I can't follow you."

Jay Webber laughed and dug her lightly in the side with his elbow. "You're my audience, baby. Ain't nobody else ever going to listen to me."

The four lanes ran out, between tourist courts, and they followed the meandering course of U.S. 321 southward as it cut across ridges and traced a stream valley—past a bucolic meadow filled with trailers, past craft shops, past a summertime carnival, past another trailer court, past service stations and a package store. Once they met a long line of traffic backed up behind a gold Cadillac traveling at thirty miles an hour, the elderly passengers staring at the passing scenery. But they were lucky. The south lane remained empty in front of them, and they made good time. Passing the Town of Blowing Rock on the bypass, Jay maneuvered along the right shoulder of the Blue Ridge, following sharp curves along a sheer drop into a valley far below.

Just as they started down the other side of the Blue Ridge, Jay cut suddenly into a little side street which shunted them off to the right. A short distance beyond, they reached a dead end in a large parking circle adjacent to a building that looked to Anna like just another craft shop. She could see they had stopped on the south slope of a steep section of the Blue Ridge because nothing but space could be seen through the small trees and shrubbery at the ends of the building.

Jay turned to her. "I'm going to show you one of nature's curiosities, Blowing Rock," he said. "It's been a landmark and a scenic attraction for generations. Back decades ago, it was free. Couples would drive up here from the Piedmont on Sundays in the '20's and '30's, even earlier in buggies. They would bring picnic lunches and spend a good part of the day courting. Now, of course, it's fenced in or fenced out, and a fee charged to visit the rock."

"What makes it so special? I mean for couples to make an all-day excursion up here. The roads must have been rather difficult back then."

"Wait until we get out on it. I mean the rock. I can show-and-tell at the same time."

They entered the gift and craft shop. Jay paid for their admission, fifty cents each, and they exited through the west end of the building. She could see immediately that the formation was not an isolated rock at all but a rock cliff, with one long spear of stone projecting at an angle higher than the bluff line and creating a center of interest. As they walked southward along the rim, she could see that the cliff face dropped only a short distance, ending on the slope of the mountain, dense with small trees and undergrowth. But the mountain itself dropped off so precipitously into the misty valley, it gave the impression of standing on the edge of a perpendicular cliff.

Just below the lip of stone was a narrow path with a railing paralleling it, making a walk along it as safe as a stroll through a meadow. At the south end of the formation a gazebo had been built on stilts out past the bluff and towered high above the tree tops on the mountain slope. A narrow walkway curved out to it.

As she stood on this observation tower and gazed almost straight down into the distant valley, then far away, along the deep gorge and across the rolling blue mountains to the west and southwest, Anna was amazed at her lack of fear. Three months ago she would have clutched the railing and closed her eyes or, more probably, would have refused to get within ten feet of the bluff rim. An almost continuous breeze swept up from below, ruffling her hair. Now and then a stronger zephyr would tug playfully at her clothes and cool her upper legs.

"That's Johns River Gorge down yonder." Jay pointed down the long valley. "Our elevation up here is a bit over four thousand feet, a good deal higher than the river. You notice the gorge bends to the right at the base of this promontory. It acts as a flume. A wind blows down it almost continuously. When it reaches the base of this mountain, instead of veering to the right, much of it is deflected upward past the rocks here. You can throw an object off, like a paper plate, and then it will be wafted back to you. Dad told me that fellows used to throw their Panama hats off and they would come back. You can stand here in the winter and watch the snow falling upward, out of the valley. That's why it's called THE Blowing Rock."

"It's fascinating," Anna said softly. "And you want to know what I wish?"

"What? I can allow you only one wish today." He turned to face her, leaning back against the railing.

"I wish I could come up here in a Model-A Ford like they did in the '30's, before the craft shop was built, and have a picnic with someone I cared for and we could throw paper plates off the rock and catch them when they blew back to us."

"*Someone* you cared for, Anna?"

"Yeah, like Pete."

He turned his back to her. "Way off yonder is Table Rock. You see it? Looks like a typical western mesa. Jules Verne used it in a science fiction novel, I think. That point beyond it is called Hawksbill. Of course that's Grandfather Mountain there to your right. You'll notice his profile is more symmetrical from an eastern view. And way, way yonder in the hazy distance—do you see that mountain peak a bit higher than the others along the skyline?"

Anna squinted. "Where? I'm not sure."

Jay placed his right arm around her neck, his forearm across her right shoulder, and pointed. "Look down my wrist and finger. See it?"

"Oh, yes. I see it now." She moved from beneath his arm.

"That's Mount Mitchell. It's the highest peak in eastern America."

"You know, I never realized that mountains this high and as numerous as these existed so close to Norfolk," she said. "I mean I knew hardly anything about the Appalachians. I never visualized so much wilderness, so much unsettled forest rolling on and on to the edge of the world. It used to surprise me when flying, to look down and see so many trees and so much empty land, after three hundred years of civilization in this country. But I never even dreamed of forests and mountains like these."

"Give us a little more time," Jay scoffed. "We the people will use it up soon enough."

Leaving the Town of Blowing Rock, they drove west on U.S. 221, following kinky curves around spurs, over ridges, and around the heads of hollows, much of the time through a tunnel of trees. Frequently, they passed jerrybuilt stands with apple or cherry cider for sale, along with honey, mountain sorghums, and other local products.

"I don't know whether it has been recorded or not," Jay Webber said out of a long silence, "but I would bet this is the crookedest highway, not just in the U.S., but on the planet earth. If follows an old Indian trail, the Yonahlossee. I've often wondered why the hell the Indians didn't take a few short cuts."

Anna laughed. "They were in no hurry, I suppose. They knew that wherever they were going would still be there unchanged, a week or a year later."

Jay shook his head. "I don't know! Somehow that doesn't explain a road this crooked to my satisfaction. Dad said the Indians followed old buffalo trails."

He was so solemn, Anna burst out laughing and laid her head against his shoulder. When he reached up with his right hand and ran his fingers through her shaggy hair, she sat up higher in her seat.

They traced a blacksnake course along the eastern base of Grandfather Mountain. At one place a sheer cliff of ancient stone reared above them. "I don't know if you are interested or not, but Grandfather and Table Rock are two of the oldest rock formations on the surface of the earth. They are quartzite, close to a billion years old. About three hundred million years ago, the day before yesterday earth time, a fantastic geological upheaval thrust them through the overlying Appalachian strata. Today, they are windows into an older, deeper layer of earth than their surface we tread upon. And, my pretty student, it is your pleasure to become acquainted with them on this bright day."

"And to pay a nominal fee for the pleasure?" Anna asked.

"Yes, inevitably, to pay a nominal fee for the pleasure."

The climb up Grandfather Mountain did not bother Anna at first. When they made the last turn to the left and started up the steepest ascent, with no trees to soften the view of the drop-off behind them, she had a terrifying feeling the the Scout was going to tip over backwards and go tumbling end over end down the slope and into the valley far below. Then she had the more plausible thought: what if the brakes should fail and the driveshaft should break. They would go careening backward, faster and faster, until Jay lost steering control and they started tumbling. She closed her eyes and clutched her hands between her knees, hoping Jay would not see her concern.

"You know, I always think, what if the brakes should give way and the driveshaft break, while climbing this slope," Jay Webber said casually. "It doesn't make any difference how often I make this climb up here—" He glanced at her. "But I ought not to scare you with your phobias."

"What? What did you say?" She stared straight ahead. "I must have been thinking of something else."

"Nothing," Jay said. "Just jabbering."

The recreational area of Grandfather lay around the "mouth and chin" area. The nose still towered high above and could be reached by climbing a ladder by those who dared the climb. There was a large parking area. Included at the visitors center was a gift shop, snack bar, museum exhibit, and an assembly hall. They walked across the "mile-high" bridge swinging above a crevasse and stood on Grandfather's chin. Jay pointed out landmarks far below. The whole world as far as Anna could see (over a hundred miles on a clear day, Jay told her) appeared to be forest-covered mountains. The more distant villages and towns and highways looked to her like grains of sand clinging to cobwebs. Only the closest places like Linville and the condominiums along the western base of the mountain were conspicuously man-made and civilized territory. From her viewpoint, the world was almost a wilderness. Anna was sure that a myopic Indian from the eighteenth century could stand there and never realize what the Paleface had done to his land only a few miles below.

Jay pointed out peaks in the great Smoky Mountains far, far to the west, on the tilting rim of the world. He showed her the Black Mountains and the Craggies. Closer by, he pointed out Brown Mountain from a different perspective. And he showed her the approximate location of some of the Piedmont cities and towns, lost in blue haze.

On the way home, they stopped at a little mountain restaurant in Linville and had a sandwich and coffee. Both were quiet. Anna had been somewhat subdued by the views from Blowing Rock and Grandfather and by height and size and concept of millennia. For some reason it made her sad. But it was not a personal sadness. It was more like the feeling she got when looking at pictures of ancient ruins and knowing that young men and women had once laughed and sung and made love there and were now nobody, nothing, particles of the elements—as though they had never been.

Chapter XIII

After the trip to Blowing Rock and Grandfather Mountain, Anna hardly saw Jay Webber for several days. He came by twice late in the afternoon, sweaty and dirty, and had a gin and tonic with her, but he did not talk much. He said something about helping out in the tobacco and if it were up to him, he would plow the damned stuff under and grow tomatoes. Anna did not question him and said little herself. She was beginning to resonate to his moods and felt she was not completely alone in the world when he was present, even if silent. Apparently, she filled some need of his at such times, she reasoned.

Then one day he showed up before lunch with Donner and Blitzen. She did not ask where they were going but rode beside him, down the spur of the ridge toward the Watauga River, speaking only occasionally. At the foot of the ridge, they cut back to the left, following the old road downriver toward Riverglade. A mass of clouds was boiling upward above the Blue Ridge, to the east behind them, and already towered from horizon to horizon almost to the zenith. It stood above the mountains like a dark, stratified Alpine cliff above the narrow valley through which they rode, threatening to tumble forward and bury them and all of Holy Rood Valley. A firey stitchwork of lightning appeared against the blackness and disappeared, followed by thunder.

Anna kept glancing back over her shoulder, feeling threatened. "Shouldn't we go back?" she asked. "I mean that storm looks ferocious."

Jay turned in his saddle and squinted skyward. "We have very few storms here from that direction. Most of ours are out of the west." He was silent a moment. "The cloud is so immense now, I can't tell what direction it's going. But if it comes this way, we can put the horses in the old barn and duck in at Riverglade."

She studied the cloud again, dubiously. "Okay, you're the weatherman. But it looks scary to me."

A short distance from the lawn at Riverglade, Jay reined his mount to the right, toward a gap in the elders, sycamores, and birch trees bordering each side of the river. Anna followed him down an old farm road to the shallows. Here, the river spread out over a wide bed of gravel and sand, forming a ford no more than two inches deep. They crossed the river, climbed the incline beyond, and left the bank growth, entering a vast alluvial bottomland, which stretched away to the foot of distant hills. Some of it was tilled, and the rest was a shimmering lake of wildflowers riding the surface of grass and weeds. The corn in a field a hundred yards away, to her left, was rich green and as tall as Anna's shoulders. Far off, to her right, a rectangular field of grain—wheat, she thought—was beginning to turn the color of Jay Webber's beard. As she looked, the tops of the grain suddenly bowed toward her as though in greeting. The next moment, a fist of wind struck her, swaying her in the saddle. Jay's mount danced sideways before the pressure. In ten seconds the wind had passed, plowing huge furrows through the wildflowers and nearby corn.

Jay looked uneasily toward the cloud, then at Anna. "There are over four hundred acres in this meadow," he said. "Eighty acres are already mine. An old lady, my father's first cousin, owns the rest. She's close to ninety now, and said I could buy her section at very reasonable terms." They were still headed straight across the fallow field, their mounts wading through Queen Anne's lace, daisies, wild asters, and ragweed. "If I could just get this land, or even half of it, I would be satisfied for life. I could raise all I would ever need for me or a family."

"Are you sure?"

He pivoted in his saddle to look at her. "What do you mean?"

"Did you ever read the Tolstoy story about the man who was promised all the land he could walk around in a day? He made his circle so wide, he ran himself to death trying to get back to his starting point before sunset."

He studied her curiously. "Do you think I'm like that, Anna?"

"Aw, silly," she laughed. "I was just teasing you."

"All I want, Anna, is enough land to grow a living on. No more. I want to live at Riverglade, marry, have a couple of kids, and live comfortably with as little work as possible for the rest of my life. Someday, I'd like to play with my grandchildren on the lawn there."

"You aren't very ambitious, are you?"

He glanced back toward the storm as another burst of wind struck them, ruffling his hair and beard. "I'm ambitious for peace and quiet and time to do the things I want to do and to spend with the ones I will love," he stated. "To me, that's the greatest of ambitions. Few millionaires are ever able to buy it."

"And you would really be content to stay in this valley and live in that old house from now on?"

"I'd prefer to live with someone I—I cared for—loved." He looked toward her again, then ahead. "And you remember this: that old house was built with loving care by those who came before me. It's comfortable and it will last."

Suddenly the sun went out as though a switch had been flipped. Jay tugged his horse to a halt and headed him toward the storm. Anna did likewise.

Overhead, the edge of the cloud had rolled past the sun, consuming it. Lightning thrust in three directions as a clap of thunder shook the world. Another wall of wind collided with them, and they were absorbed by it. Half a mile away, upstream, forest-crowned hills suddenly disappeared as a curtain of rain fell between Jay and Anna and where they sat their mounts.

"We'd better ride for it!" Jay yelled, above the wind. He wheeled his horse back toward the river and dug his heels into its sides. Anna followed him. "I didn't think about it!" he called back over his shoulder. "The way it's raining up beyond the valley, the river'll be rising right away. We'd better hurry."

Jay's horse broke into a gallop. Anna had no trouble getting Blitzen to follow. As they dashed across the field, the rising wind swept about them, tousling her hair and billowing her blouse. They plunged down the incline and into the river, already muddy and two feet deep. Although the horses were slowed by the water, they churned across, spray flying from their hooves, which beat against the gravel and rock. They climbed the grade beyond and charged into the wall of rain, as thunder bellowed close overhead. One moment Anna was dry. The next, she was wet, as though she had ridden through a waterfall.

She could see little farther than Jay and his horse, directly in front of her, and he apparently was guided by instinct. The rain gushed about her as they slowed to a trot, then to a walk. They rode out of it and beneath the shelter of the barn, before she knew they had reached its safety.

Jay swung from his saddle. "We'll turn the horses into the stables and get to the house where it's more comfortable," he called, his voice louder than necessary, now that they were out of the rain. He opened the door to a stable and turned Donner into it, closing the door.

Anna dismounted. Her wet yellow blouse clung to her body, almost transparent. Her jeans clung to her legs and were wet and sloppy, inhibiting her movement. Jay took the reins and turned Blitzen into another stall. Holding Anna by the hand, he towed her back into the storm, as they ran almost blindly toward the old mansion. Then huge hailstones were bombarding them, bounding from Anna's head and back. She covered her head with a hand in a gesture of protection.

They dashed up the steps and beneath the porch roof just as a bolt of lightning struck a tree down by the river. Anna was looking that way when a long squiggle of fire traced a path from the invisible cloud down through the rain, groping for a target. The bellow of thunder was almost deafening, rattling windows nearby. Jay opened the door, shoved her inside, and followed her. He slammed it, isolating them in a quieter refuge. Beyond the doors and walls of the house, the storm sounded farther away. Anna looked down. A puddle was forming about her feet.

"I have an idea," Jay said. "You go up to the bedroom I showed you and look in the closet. There are dresses there. Take off those wet clothes and put on a dress. I'll build a fire and dry your jeans and blouse. Now hurry up. You'll catch cold, if you don't."

"Okay, Abe MacTavish. You're the boss of Riverglade."

He smacked her on her shoulder with a loud, wet smack. "Cut the crap. It's not all that funny."

Anna hurried up the stairway and into the bedroom which once belonged to Alice and Susan Webber. Only five dresses were hanging in the huge closet. Either the wardrobe belonging to the girls had been taken after their deaths or it had been pitifully small to start with. She selected a green and red checked gingham dress and carried it over to the bed. Then she removed her wet clothes. Water traced rivulets down her naked body, especially her back, as her hair released its stored rain. She hung her panties and bra on a clothes hanger and left them in the closet. She found a terrytowel robe in the closet and used it to dry herself thoroughly. Her hair was a raggedy-ann mop, but by squeezing and toweling she managed to get most of the water out of it.

When she came back downstairs, Jay had a fire blazing in the dining room fireplace. His shoes and socks and shirt were off, but he still wore his wet trousers. He had hung the shirt over the back of a chair, near the fire, and his socks were draped across the soggy sneakers, set to one side. Steam was already curling upward from the wet socks. Anna had never seen any of his body unclothed before. His torso was as white as hers except for the constellation of russet freckles covering him and the sparse field of kinky gold hair reaching from neck to belt.

When he looked at her in the ankle-length dress, Anna saw his face soften and a pleased expression about his eyes. "You'd have made a lovely old-fashioned girl," he said. "You'd have looked even prettier in a hoopskirt."

"You just remember I've got a late twentieth century body under this old-fashioned dress," she laughed. "And I don't even have an old-fashioned brain in my head."

His face was suddenly serious. "I'll try to remember." He approached her and took her wet clothes. "Let me take these out on the porch and wring them out. They'll dry faster."

Anna was standing inside the warm radiance near the fire when Jay returned. He placed two more chairs near the fire and spread her jeans over the back of one, her blouse over the other. She noticed his trousers. They were still soaking wet, clinging to his legs.

"Can't you take your pants off and dry them

too?" she asked. "They look awfully uncomfortable on you."

He looked at her, then down at himself. "Well, no. I guess not. They're not all that wet, anyway."

"They're wet as water," she argued. "Look, Jay, when I—Don't worry about me. If you need to take your pants off and dry them, then do it."

He frowned at her. "Anna, why don't you just let me be miserable if I want to be a stupid martyr for the sake of modesty?"

She laughed and turned her back to the fire, holding her hands backward to the warmth. "It's your rear that's drowned," she retorted. "I'm warm and dry."

She heard him sigh, perhaps in exasperation, and move away toward the kitchen. Turning back, she began to watch the flames, her mind vacant. After a few minutes, she turned her back to the fire again, lifted the long skirt, and exposed the backs of her legs to the warmth the way Pete had once told her mountain women did. It felt good. She stared toward the window to her right, beyond which she could see only the white baptism of the cleansing rain as it swept past the house.

She dropped her dress hem when Jay returned, carrying a tray holding cheese, crackers, two wine glasses, and a bottle of red wine. "I thought a little snack would be in order while the storm wears itself thin," he said, his voice as cheerful as any perfect host's.

"Hey, that's splendid. When did you stash it here?" Anna seated herself on the floor, the fire on her left. She drew her heels in close to her body, and spread the long dress over her knees.

Jay sat facing her and placed the tray on the floor in front of him. He poured both glasses full of wine and handed Anna the cheese knife. She sliced off a piece of the cheese, placed it on a cracker, and nibbled at it. It was cheddar, as sharp as a tack, the way she loved it. The wine was dry and room temperature. She frowned but took another sip. She preferred her wine chilled just a mite, regardless of superficial rules. She glanced at Jay, but his eyes were on the cheese, which he was cutting. She moved her left leg because it was threatening to cramp, then realized she had exposed too much of her thigh. If Jay noticed he did not reflect it by motion or change of expression. She ignored him after that, eating in silence and sipping the wine, her mind turning to Norfolk and her job. She was accomplishing nothing here in the mountains now and found herself becoming lazy and satisfied with the slow pace of daily life.

Then she suddenly became alert. A strange sound had intruded on her thoughts. She listened. No, it was not a sound, but lack of one. The rain outside the house, the pelting against the windows and walls, had stopped as abruptly as though the faucet that controlled it had been turned off. She looked at Jay. His head was poised in a listening attitude.

"The storm's passed us," he said. "We got only the end of it, and it's moved on."

"Boy, that was quick."

"Yeah. If it had gone over us more directly, it would have dwindled out."

She listened as thunder rumbled and roared in the direction of the Blue Ridge, to the northeast. Then she became aware of another sound, a steady, muted roar much closer than the thunder. She looked at Jay.

"The river's out," he explained. "Most of the storm hit upriver, and we'll probably have a real flood." He hushed, listening. "But it probably won't last too long. After short, heavy storms like that, the water usually runs off rather quick."

"Let's go look at the river," Anna suggested. "I bet horses and cows and things will be floating down it."

Jay laughed. "Not likely. Sometimes a dead pig or chicken comes along, unless it's as bad as the one back in 1940. Mostly, it will be dead trees and brush and junk someone has left behind at a picnic."

Anna got to her feet and started toward the door. "Boy, it sounds like the Niagara Falls."

"It's still wet out there," Jay said. "I wouldn't want to interfere with your project. But if your clothes are dry, I'd put them back on if I were you."

Anna resented the suggestion for a moment, then realized the good sense in what he had said. She returned to the fireplace and checked her clothes. They were dry except for the heavy seams of her jeans. Gathering them in a bundle, she crossed the foyer to the right hand stairway and climbed the steps, returning to the room upstairs where she had found the dress. She removed it and put her clothes back on. She replaced the dress in the closet, then returned to the floor below.

Jay had dressed and waited for her in the foyer. His jeans were mottled with patches of dry and wet fabric. When he opened the front door, Anna could hear the muffled roar of the river, out of its banks, over a hundred yards away. They stepped out onto the porch. Water still ran in streams from the edge of the roof and a larger stream from each gutter where porch and house roof merged. She could glimpse swatches of muddy water at a distance through the bank growth, but the river had not risen enough to reach outside the trees.

She walked beside Jay down the steps and out the brick walk, beneath a damp blue sky. A scarf of clouds was whisked from over the sun, like a magician's trick, and the whole wet world was suddenly washed by sunlight. Millions of water drops sparkled like jewels, decorating wildflowers, weeds, and boxwood. What little hail had fallen was uncut diamonds refracting sunshine as far as Anna could see. In the northeast, the storm cloud still towered toward the dome of the sky, a genie loose from its bottle, patterns of lightning flickering across its face, followed by thunder overlapping thunder. A barely discernible rainbow glimmered against the storm, the nearer end disappearing in the trees along the river. The air she breathed and walked through was cool and humid, giving the sensation of having been cleansed and freshened—purified especially for her. The storm cloud ahead, the bright blue sky, and the blazing sun above and behind her lent a supernatural aspect to the world of Holy Rood Valley, as though Anna had gone for a walk at midnight and the sun had appeared suddenly in the sky. She looked about her in wonder and started to mention the eerie atmosphere to Jay, then thought better.

"God," Jay murmured, "it's like rising from death and finding a new world made over just for you."

"That's a weird way to put it," she said, "but it is strange—beautiful and scary."

As they came to the edge of the lawn, the roar of the river grew louder. They walked through the grass and weeds, their shoes and trouser legs saturated again almost immediately. Jay led her toward the break in the bank growth through which they had forded the stream earlier on horseback. Already, Anna could see the edge of the muddy river as it created a bay, extending an inlet up the slope past the trees and into the sunshine. The leaves of trees above the water sparkled when she moved as though made of glass.

They reached the edge of the water. Anna

could see through the tunnel of trees the crest of the main stream as the water rushed past. Logs, trash, and pieces of timber flashed by her circle of vision like frames of a film past a projector lens. The muddy water boiled and seethed, its deep liquid roar as much a part of the total atmosphere here as the sunshine itself. Poles, trash, and scraps of paper, bobbing and turning slowly, approached Anna and Jay, moved almost imperceptibly by some hidden relationship of rushing water to the still bay beneath the tunnel of trees. During the several minutes they had stood there, Anna's attention had shifted from the flotsam to the distant stream.

"What's that?" Jay Webber asked suddenly, his voice strangely tense.

The instant Anna set eyes on the object, she knew what it was, and some part of her was aware that Jay also knew. A hundred feet away, a brown oval object bobbed slowly shoreward at right angles to the rush of the river beyond. The back of the wet khaki shirt was formed into a bubble by the air trapped inside. It and the brown, saturated hair and the khaki trousers served to camouflage the corpse, floating face down toward them as though seeking their company.

"Damn!" Anna murmured.

And that was all that was said for several minutes as they stood side by side, watching the inexorable approach of the corpse. Anna's mind was blank except for one thought that kept circling round and round: how did it find me here?

"I wonder," Jay said quietly, "how it happened to wash ashore here where we are."

She looked at him but did not answer. When he started wading into the water, abruptly, without comment, she went with him. The cold water climbed past her knees as they approached the body. Jay reached down, hesitated, then grasped the upper right arm, which floated loosely. Anna took hold of the left arm. The feel of the fabric and soft, relaxed muscle beneath caused her to shudder, but she did not relax her hold. Turning as Jay turned, she walked slowly back through the chilly brown water, towing the floating corpse toward shore.

When the body began to drag against the bottom, without discussion they grasped the arms more firmly and dragged it from the water, up onto the grassy slope. It was not an easy task because the corpse weighed more than a hundred eighty pounds, exactly Pete's size, she thought fleetingly. They released the arms simultaneously and stood erect. Anna stared down at the broad shoulders and long brown hair, now lying in wet ropy strands and covering the exposed side of the face, the left side pillowed on the wet sod. Although the man had been tall, at least six feet, there was a massiveness about his legs and arms that was not concealed by sleeves and trouser legs, a suggestion of great strength. The long, delicate fingers were a stark contrast to that power.

Anna watched Jay bend slowly as though moving under water, watched him grasp the right arm of the prone figure and brace his legs, heave slowly, and turn the corpse slowly, slowly onto its left side, then suddenly onto its back. The hair fell away from the face, the handsome, ruddy face of a man who had reached the age of perhaps twenty-four. The blue eyes were the same color as the storm-washed sky, and as empty. Anna studied the thin nose and full lips, the narrow forehead. There was something weirdly familiar about the face. Her brow furrowed in puzzlement.

"Those hiking shoes are new and expensive," Jay said. "Poor fool, he was probably an amateur backpacker. His hands are as soft as yours."

"What do you suppose happened, Jay?"

"He probably got caught in the storm and slipped from a bluff or some bank, into the river. He could have gone over Dutch Creek Falls. That's happened before. He might have hit his head on a rock, but there's no sign of it."

"Poor kid," Anna sighed. "Poor young man. Somewhere, someone thinks he's alive and well."

"We've got to call the sheriff," Jay said. "He'll bring an ambulance, or call one—and the coroner, of course."

"We shouldn't leave him alone," Anna protested. "It would be a pity to leave him alone."

"Then you go. I'll stay here. The river should go down in a couple of hours, and they can cross the low-water bridge."

"No, Jay!" Anna stated emphatically. "No, you go. I want to stay with him." She felt an overpowering duty to remain with the corpse, to protect it and give it company. It was a need without reason, a duty without logic.

Jay studied her in puzzlement. "Are you sure, Anna? Do you want to be left alone with—"

Her laugh was hesitant. "This is the twentieth century, Jay. I'm not afraid of a corpse, for God's sake."

"No offense. I was just concerned for you."

"I'm sorry. I'll be fine. You go on."

He left her then and headed back toward the house.

Anna turned her back on the body, staring through the trees toward the rushing river. Looking down, she noticed a muddy little beach a foot wide, between where the water had been and where it was now and realized the river had begun to drop. The rise had been fast during the storm, at the river's head, and she supposed the fall would be even faster, with the rain over.

"You'll be okay now?"

Anna turned. Jay Webber sat on Donner twenty feet away. The horse's hooves had been muffled on the wet sod.

"Thank you, Jay. I'll be fine. Really!"

"All right. But I don't like leaving you alone here."

She smiled at him briefly, feeling a softness at the base of her throat. "You're sweet."

His eyes narrowed. He threw her a little wave of the hand, then kneed his mount forward. Donner broke into a trot, then a gallop, heading upstream.

Anna turned back, facing the inlet and the river ford, watching the water ebb and flow, swirl and eddy, carrying leaves and twigs in what looked like aimless meanderings but always, inexorably from sight among the trees, downstream, toward the far, far away Gulf of Mexico. She picked out a green sycamore leaf, called it Anna DeVoss, and watched it move first one way, then another. It looked as though it would stay in the eddy where it swirled, nothing happening to it but the same old turning and turning. But suddenly some force below the surface grasped it and whirled it away, out of sight behind a birch tree. She was so curious about what had happened to the leaf, where it was going, she almost waded back into the water in an attempt to catch sight of it.

It was at the moment she gave the leaf up to its fate that she felt the uncontrollable need to turn. She had to turn, look at the corpse. There was no escaping the command. But when she did and looked at the sprawled body, nothing had changed. It was in precisely the same position as before, the blue eyes staring back at the empty sky. Or had something changed? Something about it seemed different, as though an arm had moved slightly, or a leg, or the head had tilted a bit one way or the other.

She walked slowly to the body. Slowly, she sank to her knees in the wet grass. She studied the tranquil face, the face that would never grow older. The blue eyes were not looking at the sky, but at her. She saw far beneath the surface, within the narrow, dark wells of the pupils, a being, an entity receding into vast distances of space and time. She felt an urge to dive into those deep pupils, to stop the being, to call it back, to plead that it return.

At that moment something inside Anna DeVoss gave way. A dam broke. Great black waves of grief and frustration came pouring into her mind, into the void around her heart. Despair, locked so long behind stoic walls of routine, followed. All reason fled, leaving her a creature solely of emotion. She flung herself onto the wet chest of the dead stranger. Her arms like calipers of flesh and bone forced her hands beneath his head, forced themselves around the neck. And Anna wept. Anna wept great racking sobs which shook her body as her grief spent itself and exhausted her. She rolled her face in the curve between the jawline and neck, and her voice was the only sound on the storm-cleansed earth except for the liquid rush of the river toward the distant Gulf.

She could measure the length of her weeping only by her exhaustion. She sobbed slowly and methodically now, a quiet, controlled release of what residual grief remained in dark corners or her being. Already, the weight was missing from about her heart, which beat with a steady, normal rhythm. When she felt the arms of the corpse embrace her, she hugged the neck more firmly in return, holding her breath, her eyes tightly closed. She should have been terrified, but instead found she was at peace.

But the hand on her arm was no corpse's. It was alive and firm. It was strong. It drew her upward away from the dead body. Two hands drew her close, in an upright position. Two arms were embracing her, as Jay Webber held her close.

"Weep, my Anna," he whispered. "Get rid of it. Let it all out. It's the only way you can be free."

But her grief was mostly spent. She clung to him, not out of need, but to accommodate his kindness, and sobbed intermittently while he stroked her hair. When she thought she had cried enough to appease his concern, she withdrew from him and stepped back. Jay watched her, his eyes narrow and moist.

"Are you okay now, Anna?"

"Fine, thanks. I'm fine." She sniffled, wiped at her eyes with her fingertips. "I'll be fine now, thanks."

"I called the sheriff's office," he said. "They'll

be out here as soon as the river drops. I'll go up to the house and get a sheet to cover him—it."

"No!" Anna shook her head emphatically. "No, Jay, don't. Let the sun shine on him as long as possible. He will be in darkness long enough."

"All right, Anna." He studied her for a moment. "If that's what you want."

The sun stood just above Beech Mountain when a deputy sheriff arrived, driving down the old wagon road beside the river, followed by a rescue-squad ambulance. Anna did not feel like talking and so stood to one side, letting Jay explain to the lanky official what had happened. She watched the deputy go through the corpse's pockets and find nothing. She watched the attendants from the ambulance place it on a stretcher, carry it to the ambulance, and wheel it into the rear of the orange vehicle. She stood with Jay, quiet, watching the car and the ambulance disappear up the grassy lane.

"Let's go home," Jay said.

She let him take her by the hand and lead her back to the old barn. They mounted in silence and rode in silence up the lane and up the ridge to the DeVoss cabin. Anna dismounted and handed Blitzen's reins up to him.

"Thanks, Jay," she said. "I enjoyed the ride."

"What?"

She turned to look up at him. He was staring at her in puzzlement. "I said thanks—" She was blank for a moment, trying to think. She was suddenly exhausted. Her mind was blank. Drained. "I—I'll see you tomorrow."

"Okay, Anna. If you need me—"

"I'll ring the bell," she said.

Chapter XIV

"They sent his—the body to the pathologist at the University of North Carolina," Jay explained. "The autopsy revealed a blow to the head, but death was from drowning."

Anna stood on the deck, leaning her shoulder against a post, talking with Jay Webber, who sat on Donner in the yard. "What'll happen to—to the body now? But of course, it goes to the relatives."

"That's the strangest thing, Anna. There was no identification in his clothing. And there were no records of his fingerprints. Not even the military had records of them."

"But how could that be?" She stared at him. "He was about the right age for the tail end of the Vietnam War. He must have been subject to the draft, at least."

Jay shook his head. "Maybe he ran away to Canada and came back. Maybe he had a physical defect, a bad heart. Maybe—Who knows? There could be all kinds of reasons why there is no fingerprint record of him."

"But he looked well-to-do. Those expensive

217

shoes. He must have had a family of some means. They wouldn't just lose him."

"I don't understand it either," Jay said. "He could have been reared by some relatives who died. Or he could have grown up in some small orphanage, as far away as the West Coast. In a country this big, anything is possible. The facts are that he is dead and he is unidentified."

"Jay, what will happen to him—the body? Will they turn it over to the medical school at U.N.C.? Use it in a laboratory? I wouldn't want that. I wish we could—"

"I started to tell you," he broke in. "The damndest thing happened. The medical examiner returned the body to the sheriff's custody here. It's at the mortuary and has been embalmed. I just talked to the director this morning. He wanted me to tell him what to do with the corpse."

"That's a bit unorthodox, isn't it?" She searched his bearded face, her eyes narrowed thoughtfully. "I mean, why would they do that, return it here?"

"Search me." He shrugged, staring through the trees. "Anna, I think we ought to—"

"Jay!" she interrupted eagerly, "let's give him a decent funeral. Would your mother object if we buried him in your family cemetery?"

"I'll be darned," he chuckled. "I was just going to suggest the same thing to you. No, I'm sure Mom would not mind. She's not like that."

"That's wonderful." Anna felt suddenly clean

inside. She felt the release of a pressure she did not know she had had a moment before. "What do we do first?"

"It's simple. I'll tell the director at the mortuary. There will be some cost. I could take care of that—casket, embalming, transportation to the cemetery."

"Jay, I want to pay half of it." She watched him eagerly for an expression of consent. "May I please?"

"Sure, Anna. That would be good of you. No problem. Together we'll give the stranger a nice funeral and a grave in the mountains where he came to die. He must have loved the mountains, to hike them alone, though probably without experience."

"I'm sure he did. How could he not love them? Jay! Jay, I have another idea. It may sound crazy to you."

"No, it won't sound crazy, Anna," he said quietly. "Nothing you say sounds crazy to me. It's a good idea. We'll bury him in Sandy MacTavish's casket. I think it's waited long enough."

She stared at him in surprise, then accepted their rapport without question. "Yes, that's what I was going to suggest. And I think old Sandy would approve, if he could."

"I think so too," Jay nodded. "We'll have a simple service. We'll keep it as quiet as possible so a bunch of morbid gapers don't come cluttering up the scene, out of curiosity. Mom will insist on her minister, but I'll make him keep it brief, cut out most of the hereafter stuff. Maybe you and I could say a word or two, so he will have friends at his—his taking off."

"I agree." She paused. "I think that's the way to handle it, Jay."

It was the last Sunday in July, clear except for scattered cumulus clouds and haze in the east, stagnant pollution above the Piedmont cities. The sun stood above the green eastern hills of Holy Rood Valley, huge and orange, like the planet Jupiter seen in astronomy textbooks. In the MacTavish-Webber cemetery, a red clay hole lay open to the sky, a mound of fresh earth beside it. At the bottom of the grave, Sandy MacTavish's locust coffin rested, polished and new-looking in spite of its long years waiting in the attic of Sparr's Store. Anna DeVoss and Jay Webber had insisted that no artificial grass be spread over the mound of earth or around the grave. It was to be an honest funeral: a dead man was being interred forever in the bosom of the earth, and no pleasant euphemisms would be used. The only hitch was that Mack Jones and his boys, eager to finish the job, had lowered the coffin into the grave before the funeral ceremony.

Anna smelled the coppery fresh earth, and it stirred briefly an old sadness. Closing her eyes, she could visualize her father's broad back and the tractor he sat on as he plowed a field, several red and white chickens following in the furrow gobbling up the earthworms. She opened her eyes and was back in the cemetery.

Martha Webber, wearing a navy-blue dress and hat, stood near one end of the grave, holding Hilda's hand. Henry Sparr stood beside Mrs. Webber, dressed in a baggy wool suit which had fitted him before age had pared his flesh closer to the bones. The Reverend Joshua Larson stood next to Hilda, dressed in a white linen suit, holding a straw hat in one hand and a Bible in the other. He was a tall, lanky man, his bald head white as a boiled egg, his eyebrows, the only hair in sight, like albino caterpillars curled above his deep-set eyes. Anna, wearing the black suit she had worn at Pete's funeral, was next in line, and Jay stood to her right. He had conformed to the occasion to the extent that he wore dark trousers and a white shirt, open at the collar.

Beyond the mound of earth, several spectators gathered in a huddle for mutual security, strangers to Anna and, most of them, to each other. Some of them were dressed in neat, expensive sports clothes—summer people seeking unique entertainment. The others were dressed mostly in cheap Sunday clothes, mountain folk who lived with more important problems than what they wore. They had all merged, united by morbid curiosity. They had heard about the funeral of the drowned stranger and had come to see what would happen, to see if it would be different from other funerals they had attended. Off to one side, Mack Jones, the Webber's tenant, and two of his sons leaned on shovels, disassociating themselves from everything related to the "quare burryin," except the labor.

Reverend Larson was finishing his sermon. "We who are the quick have no way of knowing, but we pray that this young stranger was saved and that his soul will rest in the lap of our Father who art in heaven forever. Amen."

Jay Webber stepped forward. He held in his hand fertile soil Anna had seen him take from his garden, behind Riverglade. He stood close to the grave. "Although we do not know your name, you are not a stranger to Anna and me," he said quietly. "We found you and claimed you as our friend who also loved the mountains. Rest in peace, friend, here in the Appalachians, the oldest mountains on earth." He extended his hand and crumpled the dirt, letting it whisper downward. Anna could hear the soft patter against the lid of the casket. "May the rich soil of Holy Rood Valley rest with you in the peace you have found."

Anna was impressed by the simple ritual and surprised at this new side of Jay Webber. She moved forward to his side. She was confused. She wanted to say something only for the corpse, but the staring spectators beyond the grave intimidated her. She felt as though she was staging a false show just for them. Her mind cleared suddenly, and she put everything else out of her thoughts. "Young mountain walker," she said so softly only Jay could have heard her, "Rest with my husband and be remembered with equal love."

That was all. Reverend Larson turned and started shaking hands because that was all he knew to do at the end of a sermon. Mack Jones and his sons shuffled forward several feet, ready to start the task of shoveling the red clay back into the grave, so they could hurry home and get their Sunday rest. The spectators milled uncertainly, looking at each other, then back at the grave, as though expecting a Choragos to step forward and utter an epilogue; otherwise the show was hardly worth the admission—getting up early on Sunday and driving to this godforsaken cow pasture. Anna stared at them with resentment, then turned away and grasped Jay Webber's arm.

Chapter XV

Anna awakened at dawn for no reason that she was aware of. She stretched and yawned. God, but she felt good. She felt seventeen and queen of the world. And she was hungry and thirsty. She could have polished off a Roman banquet table all by herself. Dawn filtered through the windows, like square portholes in a sunken ship. She was more than hungry. Her body was famished. She kicked off the sheet and stretched her legs, her toes pointed, until her joints cracked, sounding like dead twigs broken in a silent forest. She stretched her legs far out and ran her hands along the corrugation of muscles across her stomach. "Ohoo-oo-oo!" she groaned. She hooked her right foot behind her left ankle and clamped down, muscle against muscle, with all the power she could exert, breathing hard.

She probed inside her mind. There was nothing there to disturb her. It was as clear as the spring water above the Butterfly Falls. All her needs were physical. She threw the extra pillow across the room. It landed on top of the dresser, where Pete's photograph had sat yesterday. Whose photograph?

That beautiful young stranger she had once slept with for ninety nights out of an allotted one hundred eighty-three.

She bounded to the floor, pulled her pajama top over her head, and hurried to the bathroom. Afterwards, she prepared for breakfast. Some remote segment of her mind kept listening for a knock on the door, but it never came. She ate ravenously, scrambled eggs with hot-peppered sausage mixed with them, buttered biscuits, sliced tomatoes, all with hot coffee. All three eggs would not have been enough if she had not eaten three additional biscuits, peach preserves spread between them.

After breakfast she went for a long walk out past Butterfly Falls, but the farther she got from the cabin, the more frustrated she became. The sun broke through the foliage, promising a good day, but her excursion seemed like wasted time to her. Whatever she was looking for was not out in these woods.

A new circuit came alive in her mind. She whirled in the trail and hurried back to the house. She herself had no plan, but she suspected that her body did. She dressed carefully in the prettiest white blouse and shorts she could find. After that, she applied makeup carefully, for the first time since she came to the mountains, including a green-tinted eye shadow, and fussed with her hair longer than she wanted to spend on it.

Finally, she hurried from the cabin and toward her car. The low-heeled sandals made her legs appear even longer than they were. The huge bug-eyed sunglasses gave her a sophisticated touch she believed would have turned any male's head on Granby Street in Norfolk. She drove as fast as she could take the curves up the river out of Holy Rood Valley and turned right onto the highway.

When she pulled into the parking area in front of Mark Grunwald's chalet, she stared for a moment at the white Mercedes. The night he had dated her, he had driven a black one. She wondered why he had traded, then shrugged the problem aside. When you get tired of your Mercedes, what kind of change can you make when you have everything? You trade for a Mercedes of a different color, obviously.

She got out of the car and climbed the steps to the deck. Choosing a stance she thought would look seductive, she composed her face in a whimsical little smile and rang the bell.

Nothing happened.

She rang again.

She waited a long minute.

The door whipped inward suddenly.

"Hi, Mark, I—" She shut up.

The blowsy looking dyed blonde who stood in the doorway holding a Martini in her hand was everything Mark Grunwald was not, or vice versa, she thought. The woman smiled a crooked little smile, the gin film over her eyes as bleary looking as cataracts. She thrust her head forward like a curious hen examining a new kind of bug she was about to eat and blinked at Anna.

"Mark is not heah, deah," she muttered. "I have the chalet in August. I'm the late, late Mrs. Grunwald. Are you his latest stuff?"

Anna was so startled by the question she retreated a step.

"I—I'm sorry to disturb you," Anna babbled. "I just wanted to—"

"It's all right, deah. Mark's free to mess with whomsoever he pleases. Or pleases him." She paused, turning her head to the side. "Come here, Bertha!" she called back over her shoulder.

A moment later a skinny girl of fifteen or so appeared from out of the shadows and stopped behind the blonde. She stared at Anna with large, bewildered eyes through her granny glasses. Her feet kept moving as if they wanted to rescue her, carry her somewhere away from the scene.

"Look at what your father's messin with, Bertha." The woman then laughed a guttural laugh. "Isn't she a loser compared to your mamma?"

The pain that crossed the little girl's face reflected agony and shame. Her eyes begged Anna's forgiveness.

"It's all right, Bertha," Anna said gently. "Your mother's just ill. Why don't you go on back to where you were?"

Bertha Grunwald wheeled and disappeared as quickly as she had appeared.

"Mark means nothing to me," Anna told the blonde. "But he's a gentleman. You, madam, are a shameless lush. The child should be taken from your custody, and I have a good mind to do it. I am familiar with the legal steps necessary."

The woman's face changed suddenly. Tears welled into her eyes. She thrust her hand out toward Anna. "Wait! Wait a minute, please, let me 'splain—"

Anna turned away and hurried to her car. As she was backing around to leave, she glanced back toward the front of the chalet. Mark Grunwald's ex-wife stood on the deck watching her, and she was crying.

Anna spent the rest of the day driving about the countryside. She returned to the little parking area near Linville Falls and sat for an hour listening to radio music and watching tourists come and go. She drove to Blowing Rock by way of Boone and had a Reuben sandwich and a mug of beer at Hemlock Tavern. Only tourist families came in to eat while she was there. Later, she drove about the campus at the state university in Boone and was amazed to discover that male students looked so young. She ended up at an afternoon movie, but left in the middle of it and returned to her cabin.

After a supper of tunafish salad and crackers, she got high on Martinis, the first she had had since

Pete once mixed them of Oso Negro gin, and went to bed around ten o'clock. Before the bedroom ceiling could make a tenth revolution, she was asleep, breathing softly.

She awakened abruptly and, miraculously, without a hangover. The windows were slate black. She looked at the irradiant dial on her watch. It was ten after four. Her body was a great hungry void that needed to be filled. Yet she was not hungry. She stared at the ceiling, trying to hold her mind blank. But as she stared and as she thought nothing, her left hand moved from beneath the sheet, reached out to the lid of the window seat, lifted the lid, crept stealthily down the inside of it. Her middle finger found the button of the alarm bell. She touched it gently, caressing it. She flexed her wrist to withdraw her hand, but before she could move, her finger stiffened, thrust, depressing the button once, as far as it would go. Then she snatched her hand back, letting the seat lid slam shut.

For five minutes she lay there, hardly breathing, listening, as though she expected to hear Jay Webber leaping to the floor and struggling into his clothing, way across the field. Finally, she reached out and turned on the bedside light. She removed her pajama top and crossed the room to the closet; she removed the old robe from a hanger and put it on, clutching it closed in front of her.

Then came the muted roar of an engine as it

approached the cabin, followed by a silence, then a loud knock on the door, the wrong rhythm. Anna hurried across the shadowy living room, dully illuminated from the bedroom light, and turned on the porch light. She opened the door.

"What on earth is the matter, Annar?" Martha Webber demanded. "Are you a-being bothered by somebidy?"

Anna stared at her. She stood on the deck just beyond the door, wearing a quilted robe so old it had lost all its color except a dingy gray. Her red and gray hair reached to her waist, down her back and across her shoulders. Her eyes were wide with excitement or concern, Anna could not tell which.

"Well, child, speak up! What's wrong?"

"Oh, I'm so sorry. I really am sorry," Anna stammered. "I thought I heard a noise at the door. But it was just a dog, I guess."

"Are you shore you're all right? I got to get back to Hilder. I can't leave her long by herself."

Anna looked from her to the old pickup truck in the yard. "Where's—where's Jay?"

"Lord a mercy!" She laughed, too loud for so early in the morning, Anna thought. "He done moved lock, stock, and barrel to that big old house down yander on the river three days ago. Didn't he tell you?"

"No!" Anna shook her head. "He hasn't said a word to me about moving. But I've seen him only once since the funeral."

"Well, he ort to a-told you. I got to get on back to Hilder, if you're shore you're all right."

"I'm fine. Mrs. Web—Martha," Anna said. "Thanks for coming to my rescue."

She watched the woman let herself down the steps, one slow tread at a time, as though she half expected them to break under her weight. When she heaved herself up and behind the wheel of the pickup, Anna closed the door. Hurrying back to her bedroom, she flung herself onto the bed and seized her pillow, hugging it close to her breast. "Stupid! Stupid!" she muttered.

By the afternoon of the same day, Anna decided she was going to get out of the mountains and back to where she belonged. She spent two hours packing, getting everything in greater order than necessary. By the time she had the trunk of the car loaded and the last bag buckled to the carrier rack at the rear, it was late afternoon. She reasoned that it was better to spend another night in the cabin and leave the next day. She was so tired she prepared canned soup for supper and went to bed early. But she could not sleep. She rolled and tossed for more than two hours before giving up.

She got up, finally, and mixed her a tall bloody Mary, using V-8 juice and vodka. Each time she looked at her watch, she was convinced the hands had frozen in place and could not move. At 11:00 p.m. she pulled on her jeans and a T-shirt and blundered out of the house. She got into the car, backed around, and kicked up dirt and gravel as she tore off up the driveway. She almost left the road taking the curves down the end of the ridge, then slowed, slightly sobered.

When she braked to a stop at Riverglade, she could see one dim light beyond the dining room window. Jay, barefooted and shirtless, met her at the door. He stared at her.

"Why the devil didn't you tell me you were moving down here?" Anna demanded.

"Well, I didn't think you cared. I've talked my head off trying to get you interested in the mountains, but you—"

"When I ring for your help at four—damn—o'clock in the morning and your mother shows up, I'm sure as heck interested." She pushed him aside and entered the foyer, slamming the door.

"I'm sorry, Anna. I thought it was a little cute, not telling you."

"You're about as cute as a redheaded woodpecker with a beard," she grumbled. She peered into the dining room, where a cheerful little fire burned in the fireplace. "Looks like you're having a cozy evening."

"Won't you come in and join me, your Ladyship?"

"I just felt like a little company tonight," she said. "You haven't been around lately, and I don't know anyone else."

As she approached the fireplace, Anna saw that he had spread a blanket before the fire, a pillow at one end of it. He had apparently been lying on the blanket, relaxing. How long he had intended to remain there, only he could say, if he knew himself. The blanket and pillow looked comfortable. She had a perverse urge to steal it from him, to stretch out herself and watch the fire's changing patterns. She did not admit to any right of occupation. She dropped down onto the blanket and faced the fire, her heels drawn up, hugging her knees. Jay stood and watched her for several seconds, then carried one of the ladder-backed chairs from those around the dining table over near the blanket, sitting down in it, saying nothing.

"I did not intend to run you out of your den," she said, yawning.

"No problem," he replied. "I've been using it for quite a while. I needed a change."

"Why *did* you decide all of a sudden to move down here?"

"Actually, it was not all of a sudden. I had intended to do it sometime ago. Then you came along, and I wanted to educate you in the importance of these mountains."

Anna laughed. "You mean *indoctrinate*, don't you? You ought to be a tobacco auctioneer. Or a patent medicine salesman."

He looked at her coolly. "Is that a compliment? If so, I don't really appreciate it."

"No offense." She sighed, stretched out on her back, her head on the pillow, as she watched the shadows cast by the fire dancing on the ceiling. "You were so passionate protecting the mountains from outsiders, like they were your private property."

"I was passionate, Anna. And I am. Most natives feel the same way, except the greedy ones. Do you appreciate the scenery here?"

"That's a meaningless question. Of course I do. I think things here are magnificent. I have had the most peace here I have had in the six years since Pete was listed as missing in action."

"Then visualize this, lady." He leaned forward, thrusting his head closer to her. "Visualize gaudy motels on skylines around here. Imagine the area around Boone, even here in the valley, ten years after they have four-lane highways running into them. I realize I can't change what will be. What I'm bitching about is, there's no control. Zoning is slipshod. There need to be controls. There need to be skyline laws to keep obscene commercial buildings from destroying the skylines. At the rate it's going, this country up here is going to be a red clay crater filled with tickytacky buildings instead of green mountains with a limited number of buildings. Sweet Jesus, lady, we're heading for disaster. Where will we go next when these valleys are trashed?"

Anna heard him from far away. Her mind was

shutting down. Some deep neurons were vaguely aware that he had asked her a question, but she did not know the answer yet.

"ARE YOU LISTENING TO ME, ANNA?"

At the loudness of his voice, Anna sat upright, then collapsed back onto the pillow. Then from some remote corner of her brain came the answer. "Another valley like these, until it's raped and commercialized too."

"Give the lady a silver apple!" Jay paused. "Go ahead and rest, sleep, my pretty outlander. You're already back in Norfolk. You're not interested in what I'm saying. You're still searching for Pete."

Chapter XVI

Anna awakened with a start. For a moment she was disoriented. The strange arm across her waist frightened her. Then she felt a heavy torso against her and she had a momentary need to cuddle up to it. Carefully, she moved the arm, let it slide down her front and rest on the blanket. Jay Webber's breathing changed for a moment, becoming intermittent, then long and even again.

She eased herself quietly away from him. Jay murmured. She paused, then moved again, farther backward. Finally, she stood, looking down at him. He slept peacefully. His face was relaxed and boyish despite his beard. She smiled at the spray of tiny russet freckles covering his nose. Leaning down, she kissed him lightly on the lips, their first and last kiss, she realized. She felt the silken brush of his mustache on her upper lip, the hot jet of his breath on her cheek. Straightening up, she tiptoed from the house. Her engine started quickly, and she drove up the grassy lane, away from Riverglade. She watched the massive old building dwindle into the night, in her rearview mirror, and felt a sadness she would not have suspected possible until this moment.

Back at the cabin, she went to bed, but could not sleep. For hours she tossed and rolled. The freedom she had experienced following the funeral had been compromised, but she did not understand how. Only one thing she was sure of at the moment: she had to return to Virginia Beach and to Norfolk. She got up, dressed, and finished packing a few odds and ends. The glow of false dawn was flushing the eastern rim of Holy Rood Valley when she had everything in the car. She wrote a brief note for Jay and left it beside the sink, then returned to the Porsche and started it. She sat there for several minutes listening to the smooth mutter of the engine. Abruptly, she switched it off and ran back into the cabin. She retrieved the note and carried it into the bathroom, flushing it down the commode.

Anna left the valley behind her headlights, winding her way up the river road. Dawn was a mother-of-pearl fan flecked with pink over the Piedmont, as she swung down out of the mountains, rolling from curve to curve on squealing tires. She looked forward to the comfortable apartment, to the familiar routine she had deserted weeks before. But a sadness weighed on her also. It had nothing to do with Pete DeVoss. He was dead and buried. Leaving the mountains was a special agony that startled her. Once or twice she felt a great urge to make a U-turn and head back.

She bypassed Wilkesboro in misty daylight, the coat on her tongue thick and bitter. The highway was the left lane of a planned four-lane road and was well engineered, and she encountered little traffic. The Piedmont hills unrolled beneath the Porsche's wheels like waves beneath a fast boat, as the speedometer needle crept up to eighty, then to eighty-five, before she was aware of what she was doing and let up on the accelerator.

When she saw the truck-stop ahead, she realized suddenly what she needed more than anything else—food and coffee. She slowed and whipped into the parking area, coming to a stop between a camper and a panel truck. She started to get out, then remembered the emergency toothbrush and toothpaste in the glove compartment. When the lid came open, she saw at once the neatly folded sheet of paper, one corner thrust into the slit of the small box of Kleenex. One word, *Anna,* was written on the side of the folded sheet.

Forgetting the toothbrush and toothpaste, she removed the paper from the Kleenex box and unfolded it.

Dear Mrs. Anna DeVoss:

I really liked you, to put it modestly. I "courted" you all those weeks in vain. I pretended to myself I was teaching you about the mountains, but deep down I knew I was doing it just to be with you. For a while I did hope you and I might "join forces." The episode at Riverglade during the storm and the burial of the stranger enforced my hope. But I realize now that your emotions were not concerned with me. You are too full of yourself, your grief, and your martyrdom.

I want you to understand that you are not the only one who suffered because of the Vietnam War. And your perverse martyrdom is a waste of intelligence and a waste of your potential. It is a blasphemy.

It never occurred to you to ask me anything about myself, and therefore you know nothing about me. Let me give you a few facts, my lady. I have a B.S. in Art from A.S.U. I have studied art in Italy and among the mountain Indians of Mexico. The paintings in the DeVoss cabin and the one at Riverglade are mine.

I too was in Vietnam, but I did not die quickly, without pain. Even now I won't run over a caterpillar crossing the road if I see it, yet I was compelled to cut the throats of two Vietnam soldiers while they slept to save two wounded G.I.'s. I was a medic. It took more than two years in a Veteran's hospital for me to get well enough to survive. That, and the return to the mountains. But you learned nothing about all that. Martyrs are too deep in their own grief.

I'm moving down to Riverglade. I probably

won't see you again. But I'll tell you, lady, you won't find Pete DeVoss at Virginia Beach nor at Oceana Naval Base. There's more of old Pete right here in this valley than anywhere else on earth.

So good-bye, my intelligent friend. I wish you only the best and the brightest of futures.

Jay

Anna wadded the letter into a ball and hurled it to the floor. Her eyes were filled with tears, but they were not tears of grief. She had never been so furious in her life. The smart aleck thought he knew her. She was sobbing as she started the engine. Her wheels dug in throwing gravel up under her car as she roared backward toward the asphalt highway. But at the last moment she hit her brakes and skidded to a halt. She eased backward into the highway and headed eastward at forty-five.

"The bastard," she sobbed. She dabbed at first one eye and then the other, with her fingertips. "The redheaded peckerwood! I'd like to scratch his eyes out. I'd—I'd—"

Far away, to her left, she could see the hazy bulwark of the Blue Ridge. The sun, orange and cool, stood above a line of trees in front of her. "Pete and I never did really get beyond our honeymoon!" The thought flashed across her mind like a new element through a fog chamber, startling her. "No, damn it, no! Our lives were perfect together. Our love was everything. No, you're wrong,

Jay Webber. I will have no doubts, no regrets concerning my marriage."

The green waves of the western Piedmont hills rolled beneath her at a leisurely pace. Now and then the road blurred out as though she had hit a sudden shower with the windshield wipers off. She had to blink her way back to clear visibility. "But we never went anywhere except that time to Skyline Drive and those three days with his parents in Jacksonville. Aside from that, Pete was flying, or we were at a party. No. No. Our marriage was short but sweet. If Pete had lived, if he had not been a military pilot, if we could have spent more time together—" What? What would have happened? How would it have been?

"Damn you, Jay Webber, you and your flowers and trees. I know what it was like with Pete. I was there. Me!"

She slowed to thirty-five. Wooded hills swelled into the ancient ridges of a small mountain chain to her right, a narrow creek valley to her left. The leaves, the weeds, the whole world around her, in front of her, gleamed and scintillated with the green life of earth in its early-morning robe. Clusters of blackeyed Susans and daisies decorated the grassy banks and fields around her. She saw a little island of white, where a clump of Queen Anne's lace held a family conference. Beyond them, disorganized and scattered, the tousled heads of common yarrow asserted their individualism. Yarrow has a shallow root structure, she thought. Queen Anne's lace is wild carrot. The tuber root is edible.

"Good grief, what has that kinky-headed son-of-a-gun done to me?" she muttered. "Who cares whether you can eat wild roots or not? Who really cares about the mountains and clouds and rock formations and trees? Life is back in Norfolk, where they need me."

Suddenly, she whipped into a parking area beside a faded green picnic table and braked to a halt. She threw the shift to neutral and yanked up on the emergency brake, then sat staring ahead, into the morning sunlight. Poor Pete, what an awful price to pay for the love of flying! Miles of Blue Ridge formed a miniature skyline framed by her rearview mirror. "Poor Pete!" She sighed, but it caught in her throat, choking her. "And you, Jay Webber—yes, you, you, very you! What shall I do about you?"

When she braked to a stop in front of the old mansion, Jay Webber opened the door and strolled nonchalantly toward her. She got out of the car and watched him. He came within three feet of her, stopped, and she studied his face uncertainly.

"How far did you get?" he asked casually.

"How far did I—" A surge of resentment swept over her. "What do you mean, how far did I get?"

A grin divided his red beard. "I knew I would

make you angry enough with my letter to make you challenge me, but I wasn't sure just how angry."

"Oh, so now you're a psychologist?"

"Strictly amateur, my lady."

They came together sedately, like two pawns in a foregone conclusion. He was warm and firm in her arms. She looked beyond his head, but the sky was as blue and empty as it had been that day at Oceana Naval Base when Pete's A-6 had flickered and disappeared, to rendezvous with his carrier, somewhere on the ocean beyond her vision.